"CAN I HELP YOU?"

The voice spoke from right behind her. Jenny turned—and lost her breath.

Eyes. Blue eyes. Except that they weren't just blue, they were a shade Jenny couldn't describe. The only time she'd seen a blue like that was when she once happened to wake up at the precise instant of dawn and she'd glimpsed an unbelievable, luminous color that had lasted only a second before fading to the ordinary blue of the sky.

No boy should have eyes as blue as that, and especially not surrounded by lashes so heavy they seemed to weigh his eyelids down. This boy had the most startling coloring she'd ever seen. His eyelashes were black, but his hair was white—true white, the color of frost, of tendrils of mist. He was . . . well, beautiful. But in the most exotic, uncanny way imaginable, as if he'd just stepped in from another world. Jenny's reaction was instant, total, and absolutely terrifying. She forgot Tom's existence.

Books by L.J. Smith

Available from ARCHWAY Paperbacks

THE FORBIDDEN GAME

Volume I

the Hunter

L. J. SMITH

AN ARCHWAY PAPERBACK
Published by POCKET BOOKS

New York   London   Toronto   Sydney   Tokyo   Singapore

AN ARCHWAY PAPERBACK *Original*

An Archway Paperback published by
POCKET BOOKS, a division of Simon & Schuster Inc.
1230 Avenue of the Americas, New York, NY 10020

ISBN: 0-671-87451-9

First Archway Paperback printing March 1994

10 9 8 7 6 5 4 3

AN ARCHWAY PAPERBACK and colophon are registered
trademarks of Simon & Schuster Inc.

Cover art by David Jarvis

Printed in the U.S.A.

IL 7+

For Peter, who has both feet firmly on the ground—thank heavens!

With special thanks to John Divola, for lending some of his extraordinary photographs to Zach.

the Hunter

"I told you. We have to face a different nightmare.

39

1

Jenny glanced back over her shoulder. They were still behind her, on the other side of the street but definitely following. They matched their pace to hers; when she slowed to pretend to look in a store window, they slowed, too.

There were two of them, one dressed in a black T-shirt and leather vest, with a black bandanna on his head, the other in a long flannel shirt, black-and-blue plaid, unbuttoned. Also unwashed. They both looked like trouble.

The game store was a few blocks ahead. Jenny quickened her pace a little. This wasn't the best neighborhood in town, and she'd come here specifically because she didn't want any of her friends to see her. She hadn't realized, though, that Eastman Avenue had gotten quite so rough. After the last riots the police had cleared things up, but many of the vandalized stores still had boarded windows, which gave Jenny a creeping feeling between her shoulder blades. They were like bandaged eyes turned toward her.

Not at all the place to be at dusk—but it wasn't dusk yet, Jenny told herself fiercely. If only those two guys would turn off onto another street. Her heart was beating unpleasantly hard. Maybe they *had* turned. . . .

She slowed again, her feet in their lace-up canvas Tretons making no sound on the dirty sidewalk. From behind and to the left she heard the flat smack of running shoes and the clack of bootheels. The footsteps slowed.

They were still there.

Don't look back, she told herself. Think. You have to cross over at Joshua Street to get to the store—but that means crossing left, to *their* side of the street. Bad idea, Jenny. While you're crossing they can catch up to you.

All right, then, she'd turn off before that, she'd go right on this next street up here—what was it? Montevideo. She'd go right on Montevideo, and then she'd find a store to duck into, a place to hide until the two guys had passed by.

The Tower Records on the corner of Eastman and Montevideo was no longer in business. Too bad. Back straight, stubbornly pretending she was perfectly calm, Jenny walked by the darkened windows. She caught a glimpse of herself in one of them: a slender girl with hair that Michael had once said was the color of honey in sunlight. Her eyebrows were straight, like two decisive brush strokes, and her forest-green eyes were dark as pine needles and even more serious than usual. She looked worried.

She turned right at the cross street. As soon as she

was out of sight of Eastman Avenue, she stopped and stood as still as a deer, backpack swinging from her hand, eyes desperately scanning Montevideo for cover.

Directly opposite her was a vacant lot and beside that a Thai restaurant, closed. Behind her the looming bulk of the record store presented a blank wall to the street all the way down to the park. No cover. Nowhere to hide.

Jenny's neck prickled and her little fingers began to tingle.

She turned toward Eastman and hugged the wall, tossing back her hair to listen.

Were those footsteps or just the sick thudding of her own heart?

She wished that Tom were with her.

But of course that was the whole point. Tom couldn't be with her, since it was his party she was shopping for.

It was supposed to have been a pool party. Jenny Thornton was known for her pool parties, and here in southern California late April was a perfectly reasonable time to have one. The temperature often hovered in the mid-seventies at night, and the Thornton pool glowed like a huge blue-green jewel in the backyard, giving off little wisps of steam from its surface. The perfect setting for an outdoor barbecue.

Then three days ago the cold snap had come . . . and Jenny's plans were ruined. Nobody except polar bears swam in this kind of weather.

She'd meant to rethink things, to come up with some other brilliant idea, but it had been one of *those* weeks. Summer's fourteen-year-old schnauzer had finally had to be put to sleep, and Summer had needed Jenny for moral support. Dee had taken a kung fu exam, and Jenny had gone to cheer her on. Audrey and Michael had had a fight, and Zach had had the flu. . . .

And then suddenly it had been Friday afternoon, with just hours to go before the party and everyone expecting something special—and *nothing* set up.

Fortunately an idea had come to her in the middle of computer applications class. A game. People gave murder mystery parties and Pictionary parties and things like that. Why not a game tonight? It would have to be a very special game, of course. Something chic enough for Audrey, sexy enough for Tom, and even scary, if possible, to keep Dee's interest. Something seven people could play at once.

Vague notions had run through Jenny's head of the only really exciting games she'd ever played as a child. Not the ones the adults arranged, but the kind you devised on your own once they were safely out of the house. Truth or dare and spin the bottle. Some combination of those two—only more sophisticated, of course, more suited to juniors in high school—would be ideal.

That was what had brought her to Eastman Avenue. She'd known perfectly well it wasn't the best neighborhood, but she'd figured that at least none of her friends would see her and find out about this last-minute scramble for entertainment. Jenny had gotten herself into this mess; she would get herself out of it.

Only now the mess was getting bigger than she'd bargained for.

She could definitely hear footsteps now. They sounded very close and were approaching quickly.

4

Jenny looked down Montevideo again, her mind taking in irrelevant details with obsessive precision. The record store wall was not truly blank after all. There was a mural on it, a mural of a street that looked much like Eastman Avenue before the riots. Strange—parts of the mural looked *real*. Like that storefront painted in the middle, the one with the sign Jenny couldn't quite make out. It had a door that looked real: The handle seemed three dimensional. In fact . . .

Startled, Jenny took a step toward it. The knob appeared to change shape as she moved, like any three-dimensional object. She looked more closely and found she could see the difference in texture between the wooden door and the painted concrete wall.

The door was real.

It couldn't be—but it was. There was a door stuck in the middle of the mural.

Why, Jenny didn't know. There wasn't time to wonder about it. Jenny needed to get off the street, and if this door was unlocked . . .

Impulsively she took hold of the knob.

It was cool as china and it turned in her hand. The door swung inward. Jenny could see a dimly lit room.

One instant of hesitation, then she stepped inside.

Just as she did, she consciously took in the sign above the door. It read: "More Games."

2

There was a push-button lock on the inside door-knob, and Jenny depressed it. There were no windows looking out on Montevideo, of course, so she couldn't see whether the two guys had followed her. Still, she had a tremendous feeling of relief. No one was going to find her in here.

Then she thought, More Games? She had often seen signs reading "More Books" in the arty, shabby used bookstores around here, signs with an arrow pointing up a narrow staircase to another floor. But how could there be More Games when there hadn't been any games at all yet?

Just the fact that it happened to be a game store she'd stumbled onto was strange, but very convenient. She could do her shopping while she waited for the tough guys to go away. The owner would probably be glad to have her; with that mural camouflaging the door they couldn't do much business here.

As she looked around she saw just how strange the

store really was. Even stranger than the usual odd shops around Eastman Avenue.

The room was lit by one small window and several old-fashioned lamps with stained-glass shades. There were shelves and tables and racks like any other store, but the objects on them were so exotic that Jenny felt as if she'd stepped into another world. Were they all games? They couldn't be. Jenny's mind filled suddenly with wild images from *The Arabian Nights,* images of foreign bazaars where anything—anything—might be sold. She stared around at the shelves in amazement.

God, what a weird chessboard. Triangular. Could anybody really play on a board like that? And there was another one, with strange, squat chessmen carved of rock crystal. It looked more than antique —it looked positively ancient.

So did a metalwork box covered with arabesques and inscriptions. It was made of brass or maybe bronze, decorated with gold and silver and Arabic writing. Whatever was in that box, Jenny knew she couldn't afford it.

Some of the games she could identify, like the mahogany mah-jongg table with ivory tiles spilled carelessly on the green felt top. Others, like a narrow enameled case crawling with hieroglyphics, and a red box embossed with a gold Star of David in a circle, she had never seen before. There were dice of every size and description: some twelve-sided, some shaped like pyramids, and some ordinary cubical ones made of odd materials. There were card decks fantastically colored like illuminated manuscripts.

Strangest of all, the weird antique things were intermixed with weird ultramodern things. A cork bulletin board on the back wall sported signs reading: "Flame." "Rant." "Rave." "Surf the Edge." "Cheap Thrills." Cyberpunk, Jenny thought, vaguely recognizing the terms. Maybe they sold computer games here, too. From a boom box on the counter came 120-beat-a-minute acid house music.

This, thought Jenny, is a very peculiar place.

It felt so—cut off—from everything outside. As if time didn't exist here, or ran differently somehow. Even the dusty sunlight slanting in that one window seemed wrong. Jenny would have sworn the light should have been coming from the other direction. A chill went through her.

You're mixed up, she told herself. Disoriented. And no wonder, after the day you've had—after the *week* you've had. Just concentrate on finding a game, if there's anything here that you can actually play.

There was another sign on the board, a sort of square:

```
W  E  L  C
O  M  E  T
O  M  Y  W
O  R  L  D
```

Jenny tilted her head, examining it. What did the letters say? Oh, of course, she had it now. *Welcome* . . .

"Can I help you?"

The voice spoke from right behind her. Jenny turned—and lost her breath.

Eyes. Blue eyes. Except that they weren't just blue, they were a shade Jenny couldn't describe. The only place she'd seen a blue like that was once when she'd happened to wake up at the precise instant of dawn. Then, between the window curtains, she'd glimpsed an unbelievable, luminous color, which had lasted only a second before fading to the ordinary blue of the sky.

No boy should have eyes as blue as that, and especially not surrounded by lashes so heavy they seemed to weigh his eyelids down. This boy had the most startling coloring she'd ever seen. His eyelashes were black, but his hair was white—true white, the color of frost or tendrils of mist. He was . . . well, beautiful. But in the most exotic, uncanny way imaginable, as if he'd just stepped in from another world. Jenny's reaction was instant, total, and absolutely terrifying. She forgot Tom's existence.

I didn't know people could look like that. Real people, I mean. Maybe he's not real. God, I've got to stop staring—

But she couldn't. She couldn't help herself. Those eyes were like the blue at the core of a flame. No—like a mile-deep lake set in a glacier. No . . .

The guy turned and went to the counter. The boom box clicked off. Silence roared in Jenny's ears.

"Can I help you?" he repeated, politely and indifferently.

Heat rose to Jenny's cheeks.

Ohmigod, what he must think of me.

The moment those eyes had turned away from her, she had come out of it, and now that he was farther away, she could look at him objectively. Not something from another world. Just a guy about her own age: lean, elegant, and with an unmistakable air of danger about him. His hair was white-blond, cropped close at the sides, long in back and so long over the forehead that it fell into his eyes. He was dressed all in black in a weird combination of cyberpunk and Byronic poet.

And he's still gorgeous, Jenny thought, but who cares? Honestly, you'd think I'd never seen a guy before. On Tom's birthday, too—

A flash of shame went through her. She'd better start her shopping or get out of here. The two alternatives seemed equally attractive—except that the tough guys might still be outside.

"I want to buy a game," she said, too loudly. "For a party—for my boyfriend."

He didn't even blink at the word *boyfriend;* in fact, he looked more laconic than ever. "Be my guest," he said. Then he seemed to rouse himself to make a sale. "Anything in particular?"

"Well . . ."

"How about Senet, the Egyptian Game of the Dead?" he said, nodding at the enameled case with the hieroglyphics. "Or the I-ching? Or maybe you'd like to cast the runes." He picked up a leather cup and shook it suggestively. There was a sound like rattling bones.

"No, nothing like that." Jenny was feeling distinctly unnerved. She couldn't put her finger on it, but something about this guy sent whispers of alarm through her blood. Maybe it was time to go.

"Well—there's always the ancient Tibetan game of goats and tigers." He gestured at a curiously carved bronze board with tiny figurines on it. "The fierce tigers, see, stalk the innocent little goats, and the innocent little goats try to run from the tigers. For two players."

"I—no." Was he making fun of her? There was something to the twist of his mouth that made Jenny think yes. With dignity she said, "I was looking for—just a game that a lot of people can play at once. Like Pictionary or Outburst," she added defiantly. "But since you don't seem to have anything like that in the store—"

"I see," he said. "That kind of game." Suddenly, looking at her sideways, he smiled. The smile unnerved Jenny more than anything yet.

Definitely time to go, she thought. She didn't care whether the tough guys were still outside. "Thank you," she said with automatic politeness, and she turned to the door.

"Mystery," he said. His voice caught Jenny halfway across the room. She hesitated in spite of herself. What on earth did he mean?

"Danger. Seduction. Fear." Jenny turned back to face him, staring. There was something almost mesmerizing about his voice—it was full of elemental music, like water running over rock. "Secrets revealed. Desires unveiled." He smiled at her and pronounced the last word distinctly: "Temptation."

"What are you talking about?" she said, tensed to hit him or run if he took one step toward her.

He didn't. His eyes were as innocently blue as Nordic fjords. "The Game, of course. That's what you want, isn't it? Something . . . very special."

Something very special.

Exactly what she'd thought herself.

"I think," she said slowly, "that I'd better—"

"We do have something like that in stock," he said. Now's your chance, she told herself when he

11

disappeared through a door into the back room. You can just walk out of here. And she was *going* to leave, she was just about to go, when he appeared again.

"I think," he said, "that this is what you've been looking for."

She looked at what he was holding, then up at his face.

"You've got to be joking," she said.

The box was about the size and shape of a Monopoly game. It was white and glossy and there wasn't a single word, line, or figure printed on it.

A blank white box.

Jenny waited for the punch line.

There was something about it, though. The more she looked at that box, the more she felt . . .

"Could I see it?" she said. Touch it, was what she meant. For some reason she wanted to feel the weight of it in her hands, the sharpness of its corners in her palms. It was silly, but she did want to. She *really* wanted to.

The guy leaned back, tilting the box between his own hands, gazing at its glossy top. Jenny noticed that there wasn't a single fingerprint on the shiny finish, not so much as a smudge. She also noticed that his fingers were long and slender. And that he had a snake tattooed on his right wrist.

"Well . . ." he said. "I don't know. On second thought, I'm not sure I can sell it to you after all."

"Why *not?*"

"Because it really is special. Un-mundane. I can't let it go to just anybody, or for just any reason. Maybe if you explained what it was for. . . ."

Why, he's a tease, Jenny thought. Without in the least stopping being scared, or disturbed, or any of the other things she'd been since she'd come into this store, she started being amused as well. Wildly, inexplicably amused.

Maybe if I looked like him, was that gorgeous, I'd be a tease, too, she thought. She said seriously, "It's for a party tonight, for my boyfriend, Tom. He's seventeen today. Tomorrow night we'll have the big party—you know, with *everybody* invited, but tonight it's just our group. Our crowd."

He tilted his head to one side. Light flashed off the earring he was wearing—a dagger or a snake, Jenny couldn't tell which. "So?"

"So I need something for us to do. You can't just get seven people in a room, throw Doritos at them, and expect them to have a good time. I've screwed up *massively* by not getting organized until now—no real food, no decorations. And Tom—"

The guy tilted the box again. Jenny watched its surface turn milky, then bright, then milky again. It was almost hypnotic. "And Tom will care?" he said, as if not believing it.

Jenny felt defensive. "I don't know—he might be disappointed. He *deserves* better, you see," she added quickly. "He's—" Oh, how to explain Tom Locke? "He's—well, he's incredibly handsome, and by the end of this year he'll have lettered in three sports—"

"I get it."

"No, you don't," Jenny said, horrified. "He's not like that at all. Tom is *wonderful*. He's just—*so* wonderful that sometimes it takes a little keeping up with him. And we've been together forever, and I love him, and I have since second grade. Okay?" Anger gave her courage, and she advanced a step

13

toward the guy. "He is absolutely the best boyfriend in the world, and anybody who says he isn't—"

She stopped. The boy was holding out the box to her. Jenny hesitated, nonplussed.

"You can hold it if you want," he said gently.

"Okay," Jenny said, embarrassed, her vehemence fading. She took the glossy box gingerly between her palms—and forgot everything else. It was cool and just weighty enough to be intriguing. Something inside rattled slightly, mysteriously. There was a quality about it that Jenny couldn't describe, a sort of electric current that ran up her fingers as she held it.

"We're closing," the boy said briskly, with another of his arbitrary mood swings. "You gonna buy it?"

She was. She knew perfectly well anybody crazy enough to buy a box without looking inside it deserved whatever they got, but she didn't care. She wanted it, and she felt a strange reluctance to take the lid off and peek in. No matter what, this would make a great story to tell Tom and the others tonight. *The craziest thing happened to me today. . . ."*

"How much?" she asked.

He went to the counter and hit a key on an antique-looking brass cash register. "Call it twenty."

Jenny paid. She noticed the cash drawer was full of odd-looking money all jumbled together: square coins, coins with holes in the center, crumpled bills in pastel colors. The wrongness of that cut into her pleasure in the box a little, and she felt another chill, like spiders walking on gooseflesh.

When she looked up, the boy was smiling at her.

"Enjoy," he said, and then his heavy lashes drooped as if at a private joke.

From somewhere a clock chimed the little unfinished tune that meant half past some hour. Jenny glanced down at her watch and stiffened in horror.

Seven-thirty—it couldn't be! There was no way she could have been in this store for over an hour, but it was true.

"Thank you; I have to go," she gasped distractedly, heading for the door. "Uh—see you later."

It was just a politeness, not meant to be answered, but he did answer. He murmured what sounded like "at nine" but undoubtedly was "that's fine" or something like that.

When she looked back, he was standing half in shadow, with the stained glass of a lamp throwing blue and purple stripes on his hair. For just a second she caught something in his eyes—a *hungry* look. A look completely at odds with the indifferent manner he'd worn while speaking to her. Like—a starving tiger about to go hunting. It shocked Jenny so much that her "goodbye" froze in her throat.

Then it was gone. The boy in black reached over and turned the acid house music on.

Terrific soundproofing, Jenny thought as the door closed behind her and the music was cut off. She gave herself a mental shake, throwing off the lingering image of those blue eyes. Now if she *ran* all the way home, she might just have time to throw some Cheez Whiz in the microwave and shove a handful of CDs in the player. Oh, God, what a day!

That was when she noticed the tough guys.

They were waiting for her across the street, hidden in the blue-gray shadows of dusk. Jenny saw them coming and felt a jolt to her stomach. Swiftly and automatically she stepped backward, reaching behind her for the doorknob. Where *was* it? And why was she so stupid today? She should have asked the guy in black if she could use the phone; she should have called Tom—or Dee— *Where was the knob?*

They were close enough that she could see that the one in the flannel shirt had bad skin. The one with the bandanna was grinning in a very creepy way. They were both coming toward her *and where was the freaking doorknob?* All she could feel behind her was cool, painted concrete.

Where is it where is it—

Throw the box at them, she thought, suddenly calm and clear. Throw it and run. Maybe they'll stop to investigate it. Her mind, utterly practical, ordered her hand to stop searching for a doorknob that wasn't there. Waste of time.

With both hands she lifted the white box to throw it. She wasn't sure exactly what happened next. Both guys stared at her and then—they turned around and started running.

Running. Flannels was in the lead, and Bandanna just a length behind him, and they were running like deer, with an animal grace and economy of motion. Fast.

And Jenny hadn't thrown the box after all.

My fingers . . . I didn't throw the box because I couldn't let go because my fingers . . .

Shut up, her mind told her. If you're dumb enough to care more about a box than about your own life, okay, but at least we don't have to dwell on the subject.

Walking quickly, sweatered arms cradling the box to her chest, she started for home.

She didn't turn around to see how she'd missed the

doorknob with all her behind-the-back fumbling. At the time she simply forgot.

It was ten to eight when Jenny finally neared her street. The lighted living rooms in the houses she passed looked cozy. She was out in the chill dark.

Somewhere on the way home she'd started to have misgivings about the game. Her mother always said she was too impulsive. Now she'd bought this— thing—without even knowing exactly what was inside. Even as she thought it, the box seemed to thrum slightly in her arms as if charged with hidden power.

Don't be silly. It's a box.

But those guys *ran,* something whispered in the back of her mind. Those guys were *spooked.*

As soon as she got home, she was going to check this game out. Examine it thoroughly.

A wind had sprung up and was moving the trees on Mariposa Street. Jenny lived in a sprawling ranch-style house set among those trees. As she approached it, something slunk furtively by the front doorway. A shadow—a small one.

Jenny felt a prickling at the back of her neck.

Then the shadow moved under the porch light and turned into the ugliest cat in America. Its fur was mottled gray and cream (like a case of mange, Michael said), and its left eye had a permanent squint. Jenny had taken it in a year ago, and it was still wild.

"Hey, Cosette," Jenny said, darting forward and petting the cat as relief swept through her. I'm really getting jumpy, she thought, scared by every little shadow.

Cosette put her ears back and growled like the

17

possessed girl in *The Exorcist.* She didn't bite, though. Animals never bit Jenny.

Once in the front hallway Jenny sniffed suspiciously. Sesame oil? Her parents were supposed to be leaving for the weekend. If they'd changed their minds . . .

Alarmed, she dumped her backpack—and the white box—on the living room coffee table as she galloped to the kitchen.

"At last! We were beginning to think you weren't coming."

Jenny stared. The girl who'd spoken was wearing an army fatigue jacket and sitting on the counter, one incredibly long leg braced on Jenny's mother's blondwood kitchen table, the other dangling. Her hair was cropped so close to her head it looked like little nubs of black velvet on her skull. She was as beautiful as an African priestess, and she was grinning wickedly.

"Dee . . ." Jenny began.

The other inhabitant of the kitchen was wearing a black-and-white houndstooth-check jacket and Chanel earrings. Around her was spread a sea of utensils and ingredients: metal cleavers and ladles, eggs, a can of bamboo shoots, a bottle of rice wine. A wok was sizzling on the stove.

". . . and Audrey!" Jenny said. "What are you *doing* here?"

"Saving your butt," Audrey answered calmly.

"But—you're cooking!"

"Of course. Why shouldn't I cook? When Daddy was assigned to Hong Kong we had a chef who was like part of the family; he used to talk Cantonese to me while Daddy was working and Mother was at the beauty parlor. I loved him. Naturally I can cook."

While this speech was going on, Jenny was looking back and forth from one girl to the other. When it was over she burst into laughter, shaking her head. Of course. She should have known she couldn't fool these two. They must have seen that under her facade of self-confidence about the party she was frantic. They knew her far too well—and they'd come to rescue her. Impulsively Jenny hugged each of them in turn.

"Since Tom loves Chinese, I decided to take care of the food," Audrey went on, dropping something dumplinglike into the wok. "But where have you been, hmm? Run into some kind of trouble?"

"Oh—no," Jenny said. If she explained what had happened, she'd just get yelled at for going into a bad neighborhood. Not by Dee, of course—Deirdre Eliade's recklessness was matched only by her somewhat skewed sense of humor—but by the ever-practical Audrey Myers. "I was just buying a game for tonight—but I don't know if we're going to need it after all."

"Why not?"

"Well . . ." Jenny didn't want to explain that, either. She didn't know *how* to explain it. She only knew she needed to look at that box before anyone else arrived. "It might be boring. So what are you making?" She peered into the wok to change the subject.

"Oh, just some *Mu shu rou* and a few *Hei jiao niu liu.*" Audrey was moving around the kitchen with her usual mannered grace, her tailored clothes unmarred by a single spot of grease. "That's stir-fried pork and spring rolls to you provincial types. Also fried rice and the trimmings."

"Pork," said Dee, taking a leisurely sip of Carbo Force, her favorite energy drink, "is death on wheels. You have to lift at the gym for a week to work off one pork chop."

"Tom loves it," Audrey said shortly. "And he looks all right."

Dee gave a maddening laugh, and hostility flashed across the room like lightning.

Jenny sighed. "Oh, get over it. Can't you call a truce for just one day in the year?"

"I don't *think* so," Audrey hummed, expertly fishing a spring roll out of the wok with chopsticks.

Dee's teeth flashed white in her night-dark face. "And ruin a perfect record?" she said.

"Look, I am not going to have Tom's party ruined —not even by my two best friends. Understand?"

"Oh, go to your room and become beautiful," Audrey said indulgently and picked up a cleaver.

The box, thought Jenny—but she did have to change her clothes. She'd better make it fast.

3

In her room Jenny exchanged her crewneck sweater and jeans for a flowing cream-colored skirt, a tissue-linen blouse, and a beaded batik vest that glowed with hundreds of tiny golden threads.

Her eyes were drawn to a stuffed white rabbit on the dresser. The rabbit was holding a daisy with the words *I love you* emblazoned across its center. An Easter gift from Tom, a ridiculous thing, but one she knew she would keep forever. The fact that he wouldn't say the words in public just made this secret confession all the sweeter.

For as long as she could remember, she had been terribly in love with Tom. Whenever she thought of him, it was like a sudden quick ache, a sweetness almost too much to bear. She felt it in various places in her body, but it was an emotional thing, mainly, and centered in her chest. It had been that way since second grade. Stuck around the frame of the mirror were pictures of them together—at the sixth-grade

Halloween Hop (in costume), at the ninth-grade graduation dance, at the junior prom two weeks ago, at the beach. They had been a couple for so long that everyone thought of them as Tom-and-Jenny, a single unit.

As always, the very image of Tom seemed to wrap a thin blanket of comfort over her. This time, though, Jenny felt something nagging at her underneath the comfort. Something tugging at her to think about it.

The box again.

Okay, go look at it. Then think *party*.

She was dragging a brush through her hair when there was a perfunctory tap at the door and Audrey came in.

"The spring rolls are finished and the stir-fry has to wait till the last minute." Audrey's own hair, which she always wore up, was glossy auburn, almost copper. Her eyes were chestnut and just now narrowed in disapproval. "New skirt, I see," she added. "A long one."

Jenny winced. Tom liked her in long skirts, especially the soft and flowing kind. Audrey knew it and Jenny knew she knew it. "So?" she said dangerously.

Audrey sighed. "Can't you see? You're letting him get too sure of you."

"Audrey, please—"

"There's such a thing as being too good," Audrey said firmly. "Listen to me, because I *know*. Guys are weird, *n'est-ce pas?* You never want one to be that sure of you."

"Don't be ridiculous," Jenny began, then stopped. For some reason, for just a second, she thought of the guy at the game store. Eyes as blue as the core of a flame.

"I'm serious," Audrey was saying, her head tilted back to look at Jenny through spiky jet-black eyelashes that touched equally spiky copper bangs. "If a guy feels too secure, you lose his attention, he takes you for granted. Starts looking at other girls. You want to keep him off balance, never knowing what you'll do next."

"Like you do with Michael," Jenny said absently.

"Oh, Michael." Audrey made a dismissive gesture with exquisitely polished nails. "He's just keeping the seat warm until I decide who's next. He's a—a bookmark. But do you see what I'm saying? Even Dee thinks you give in to Tom too much."

"Dee?" Jenny raised her eyebrows ironically. "Dee thinks all guys are lying hounds. As boyfriends, anyway."

"True," said Audrey. "It's strange," she added thoughtfully, "how she can be so right about that and so wrong about everything else."

Jenny just made a wry face at her. Then she said, "You know, Audrey, maybe if *you* tried being nice first—"

"Hmm, maybe . . . when the devil goes ice-skating," Audrey said.

Jenny sighed. Audrey was the newcomer to their group; she'd moved to Vista Grande last year. All the others had known each other since elementary school, and Dee had known Jenny longest of all. When Audrey arrived, Dee had gotten—well, jealous. They'd been fighting ever since.

"Just try not to kill each other during the party," Jenny said. Deliberately she pulled her hair back—

23

the way Tom liked it—and anchored its silkiness with an elastic band.

Then she smiled at Audrey and said, "Let's go back to the kitchen."

When they did they found that Michael and Zach had arrived—looking, as usual, as different as night and day.

Michael Cohen was shaped like a teddy bear, with dark hair as rumpled as his gray sweats and the eyes of a sarcastic spaniel. Zach Taylor had light hair pulled back in a casual ponytail, an intense beaky-nosed face, and eyes as gray as the winter sky.

"How's the flu?" Jenny said, kissing Zachary's cheek. She could do this safely because she'd been exposed to his germs all week, and besides, he was her cousin. Zach's gray eyes softened for just an instant, then went cool again. Jenny was never quite sure if Zach liked her or merely tolerated her the way he did everyone else.

"Hello, Michael," she said, giving him a pat instead of a kiss. The liquid spaniel eyes turned toward her.

"You know," Michael said, "sometimes I worry about us, about our whole generation. Do we know what we're doing? Are we any better than the Me Generation? What do we have to look forward to, except driving better cars than our parents? I mean, what is the *point?*"

"Hello, Michael," said Audrey.

"Hello, O light of my life. Is this an egg roll I see before me?" Michael said, reaching.

"Don't eat that. Put it back on the plate with the others and take it out to the living room."

"I live to serve," Michael said and departed.

God—the box, Jenny thought. Michael was the sort who would potter around the room reading your mail and opening your drawers in an absentminded way. Insatiably curious. She followed him.

Her stomach knotted at the sight of it, pristine and rectangular and gleaming on her mother's solid ponderosa pine coffee table. Jenny's mother had worked very hard with a very expensive decorator to make sure the living room looked "natural and inevitable and not at all arty." There were Navajo weavings and Hopi baskets on the walls, Zuni pots on the floor, and a Chimayo rug above the fireplace. Jenny wasn't allowed to touch any of them.

Calm down, she told herself. But even approaching the white box was strangely difficult. She picked it up and realized that her palms were sweaty enough to stick to it.

Thrummm. The current tingled through her fingers. The feeling of something wrong increased.

Oh, hell! I'll just throw the thing away, Jenny thought, surprised at the relief the idea brought. We'll play canasta.

Michael, munching spring rolls, was eyeing her with interest.

"What's that? A present?"

"No—just a game I bought, but I'm going to get rid of it. Michael, do you know how to play canasta?"

"Nope. So where's the sun bunny?"

"Not here yet—oh, that's probably her. Would you get the door?"

Michael just looked vaguely at the plate in his one hand and the roll in his other. Jenny ran to the hallway, still holding the box.

Summer Parker-Pearson was tiny, with thistledown hair and dimples you wanted to poke your fingers into. She was wearing a china blue shirtdress and shivering.

"It's freezing out here. How're we going to go swimming, Jenny?"

"We're not," Jenny said gently.

"Oh. Then why did I bring my bathing suit? Here's my present." She piled a shirt box wrapped in maroon paper on top of the white box Jenny was holding, added a small tote bag to the stack, and headed for the living room.

Jenny followed, put all the things on the coffee table, then pulled the white box from beneath them. *Thrum.* Summer was saying hello to Mike and Zach and Dee.

"Look," Jenny said, "if you guys will excuse me for a second—" She was cut off by the doorbell. This time she didn't want anybody else to answer it. "I'll get it."

Tom was on the doorstep.

He looked good. Of course, he always looked good to Jenny, but tonight he was especially handsome, really *devilishly* good-looking, with his dark brown hair neat and short and his smile faintly mocking. Tom wore simple clothes like other guys, but somehow he wore them differently. He could make a pair of Basic Jeans look as if they'd been tailored for him. Tonight he was wearing a teal T-shirt under a buttondown shirt that was simply a beautiful blue, an intense color that reminded Jenny of something.

"Hi," Jenny said.

He grinned rakishly and held out an arm to her.

26

Jenny went willingly, as always, but she hung on to the box. "Tom, there's something I want to talk to you about, alone. It's hard to explain—"

"Oh, no, I'm getting 'Dear Johnned' on my birthday," he said loudly, arm still around her, leading her down the hallway to the living room.

"Quit it," Jenny said, exasperated. "Can you please be serious for a minute?"

Tom was clearly in no mood to be serious. He waltzed her into the living room, where everyone but Audrey was sitting around laughing and talking. He ignored her protests, which were growing fainter anyway. Tom always made Jenny feel better, and it was hard to stay worried with him around. All her fears of shadows and thrumming boxes seemed faraway and childish.

Still, she felt a prickle of unease as he took the box from her, asking, "What's this? For me?"

"It's a game," Michael said, "about which Jenny's being very mysterious. She can't let go of it, apparently."

"I understand why," Tom said as he shook the box to hear the rattle. Jenny looked at him sharply. He didn't seem to be joking, or at least no more than usual, but how could you say that about a blank white box? Why should Tom look so deeply intrigued by it, shifting it in his hands eagerly?

There *is* something about it, Jenny thought, opening her mouth to speak. But just then her mother came in from the back of the house, fastening an earring and wafting perfume. Jenny shut her mouth again.

Mrs. Thornton had been blond like Jenny when

she was young, but over the years her hair had darkened to a golden brown, honey-in-shadow tone. She smiled at everyone and said happy birthday to Tom. "Now, let me see," she said to Jenny, "Joey's out of the way at the Stensons', and we'll be back late Sunday, so everything should be ready for you."

Then, as Jenny's father appeared behind her with a small suitcase, she added earnestly, "Dear one, I know you're going to break *something*. Just don't let it be the R. C. Gorman vase, all right? It cost fifteen hundred dollars, and your father is deeply attached to it. Otherwise, clean up whatever you destroy and try to keep the roof on."

"If it comes off, we'll nail it back," Jenny promised, then kissed her mother's smooth Shalimar-scented cheek without embarrassment.

"Krazy Glue in the kitchen drawer," Jenny's father muttered in her ear as she kissed him in turn. "But watch out for the R. C. Gorman vase. Your mother would die."

"We won't go near it," Jenny said.

"And no . . ." Her father made a vague fiddling gesture with one hand. He was looking at Tom in a way that Jenny thought was what people meant when they said *askance*. He'd taken to looking like that at Tom lately.

"Daddy!"

"You know what I mean. Only the girls are staying the night, right?"

"Of course."

"Right." Her father pushed his wire-framed glasses higher on his nose, squared his shoulders, and looked at her mother. They both glanced around the living room one last time—as if to remember it—

and then, like a pair of fatalistic soldiers, they turned and marched out the door.

"Don't have much faith in us, do they?" Michael said, looking after them.

"It's the first time I've had a party while they've been away for the weekend," said Jenny. "That they know about," she added thoughtfully.

When she looked back, Tom had the box open.

"Oh—" Jenny said. And that was all she said. Because Tom was lifting out sheets of thick, glossy tagboard, printed in colors so vibrant they glowed. Jenny saw doors and windows, a porch, a turret. Shingles.

"It's a dollhouse," said Summer. "No, I mean one of those paper thingies, like you get in the big flat books and cut out. A paper house."

Not a game, Jenny thought. And not dangerous. Just a kids' toy. She felt a wave of relaxation soften her, and when Audrey called from the kitchen that the food was ready, she went almost dreamily.

Tom was suitably surprised and impressed at the Chinese dinner, and the fact that Audrey was responsible for it.

"You can cook!"

"Of course I can cook. Why is it that everyone assumes I'm a mere social ornament?" She looked at him from under spiky lashes and smiled.

Tom smiled back, maintaining eye contact. Audrey kept flirting as she served him, smiling up at him, allowing her fingers to touch his as she handed him a plate. But when he moved away, she slanted a grim, significant glance at Jenny. *You see?* that glance said.

Jenny returned the look benevolently. Tom was

always nice to other girls, and it didn't bother her. It didn't mean anything. She was feeling very pleased with the world as they all filled their plates and went back to the living room.

There was no formal dining. They all sat around the coffee table, some on leather footstools, some directly on the Mexican paver tiles. Jenny was surprised that the white box with the sheets of tagboard wasn't already put aside.

"You got some scissors?" asked Zach. "Actually, an X-Acto knife would be better. And a metal ruler, and glue."

Jenny stared at him. "You're going to *make* it?"

"Sure, why not? It looks like a good model."

"It's cute," Summer said and giggled.

"You've got to be kidding," Jenny said. "A paper house . . ." She looked around for support.

"It's a game," Dee said. "See, there are instructions on the back of the lid. Scary instructions." She shot a barbaric smile around the room. "I like them."

Michael, with bits of spring roll hanging out of his mouth, looked alarmed.

"But how can you play a *game* with a paper house?" Jenny felt her voice going weak again as she saw the way Tom was looking at her. The way only Tom could look—charming, persuasive, and tragic. It was all a put-on, but Jenny could never resist. "Oh, all right, you big baby," she said. "If you really want it. I should have gotten you a rattle and a pacifier, too." Shaking her head, she went off to fetch the scissors.

They put the model together as they ate, occasionally getting grease on the tagboard, gesturing with chopsticks. Tom supervised, naturally. Zach did a lot of the cutting; he'd had practice matting the photographs he took. Jenny watched his careful, clever fingers transform the flat sheets of paper into a three-foot-high Victorian house and was forced into admiration.

It had three floors and a turret and was open in front like a dollhouse. The roof was removable. Sheet after sheet had to be cut out to make all the chimneys and cornices and balconies and eaves, but no one got tired of working, and only Michael complained. Tom seemed delighted with the whole thing. Even Audrey, whom Jenny would have thought far too sophisticated to enjoy this, lent an experienced hand.

"Look, here's some furniture to put inside—are you done with the first floor, Zach? You see, this is the parlor, and here's a little parlor table. Gothic Revival, I think. Mother has one. I'll put it . . . here."

"Here's a sort of Oriental screen thing," Summer said. "I'll put it by the table for the dolls to look at."

"There aren't any dolls," said Jenny.

"Yes, there are," Dee said and grinned. She'd curled her long legs up and was reading the instructions to herself. "And they're *us*. It says we each get a paper doll for a playing piece, and we draw our own face on it, and then we move the pieces through the house, trying to get to the turret at the top. That's the game."

"You said it was scary," Tom objected.

"I didn't finish. It's a haunted house. You run into

a different nightmare in every room while you're trying to get to the top. And you have to watch out for the Shadow Man."

"The *what?*" Jenny said.

"The Shadow Man. He's like the Sandman, only he brings you nightmares. He's lurking around inside, and if he catches you, he'll—well, listen. He'll 'bring to life your darkest fantasies and make you confess your most secret fears,'" she read with obvious enjoyment.

"*All right!*" said Tom.

"Oh, geez," said Michael.

"What kind of darkest fantasies?" said Summer.

Mystery, thought Jenny. Danger. Seduction. Fear. Secrets revealed. Desires unveiled.

Temptation.

"What's wrong with you, Thorny?" Tom said affectionately. "You're so nervous."

"It's just—I don't know if I like this game." Jenny looked up at him. "But you do, don't you?"

"Sure." His hazel eyes, brown flecked with green, were sparkling. "It's good for a laugh." Then he added, "Don't be scared. I'll protect you."

Jenny gave him a mock glare and leaned against him. When she was away from Tom, the skin of her forearm missed him, and so did her shoulder and her side and her hip. The right side because she always sat on Tom's left.

"Go get some of Joey's crayons," Dee was ordering Summer. "We're going to need to draw a lot. Not just the paper dolls that are us; we're also supposed to draw our worst nightmare."

"Why?" said Michael unhappily.

"I told you. We have to face a different nightmare

in every room. So we each draw one on a slip of paper and shuffle the papers and put them facedown on the floor of different rooms. Then when you get to a room, you can look at the slip and see what that person's nightmare is."

Tom wiped his fingers on his jeans and went to sit by Dee on the couch, bending his head over the instructions. Summer jumped up to get crayons from Jenny's little brother's room. Zach, ignoring the rest of them, was working silently. Zach didn't say anything unless he had something to say.

"I think I'm going to like this," Audrey said, judiciously placing furniture in the different rooms. She was humming a little, her polished nails gleaming, her hair shining copper under the track lighting.

"Here are the crayons, and I found some colored pencils, too," Summer said, returning with a Tupperware container. "Now we can all draw." She rummaged through the sheets of glossy tagboard left in the box, finally producing one printed with human outlines. The paper dolls.

They were all enjoying themselves. The game was a hit, the party a success. Jenny still felt cold inside.

She had to admit, though, that there was a certain satisfaction in cutting neatly along dotted lines. It brought back long-ago memories. Coloring the paper dolls was fun, too, the Crayola wax sliding richly onto the stiff matte tagboard.

But when it came to drawing on the rectangle of paper Summer gave her next, she stopped helplessly.

Draw a nightmare? Her worst nightmare? She couldn't.

Because the truth was that Jenny had a nightmare. Her own, personal, particular nightmare, based on something that had happened long ago ... and she couldn't remember it. She could never remember it when she was awake.

The bad feeling was coming on, the one she sometimes got late at night. The scared feeling. Was she the only person in the world who woke up in the middle of the night sure that she'd discovered some awful secret—only, once she'd awakened, she couldn't remember what it was? Who felt sick with fear over something she couldn't remember?

A picture flickered through her mind. Her grandfather. Her mother's father. Thinning white hair, a kind face, tired, twinkling dark eyes. He had entertained her when she was five years old with souvenirs from far-off places and magic tricks that had seemed real to a child. His basement had been full of the most wonderful things. Until the day something had happened. . . .

That last horrible day . . .

The flicker died, and Jenny was glad. The only thing worse than not remembering was remembering. It was better to just leave the whole thing buried. The therapists had said differently at the time, but what did they know?

Anyway, she certainly couldn't draw it.

The others were all sketching assiduously. Tom and Dee were snickering together, using the lid of the game box as a desk. Summer was laughing, shaking back her soft light curls, drawing something with a lot of different colors. Zach was frowning over his nightmare, his face even more intense than usual; Audrey's eyebrows were arched in amusement.

"Where's green? I need lots of green," said Michael, hunting among the crayons.

"What for?" asked Audrey, eyes narrowed.

"Can't tell you. It's a secret."

Audrey turned her back on him, shielding her own paper.

"That's right, they're secrets," Dee agreed. "You don't get to see them until you reach the room they're in."

Nobody here could possibly have a secret from me, Jenny thought. Except Audrey, I've known them all forever. I know when they lost their first tooth and got their first bra. None of them could have a real secret—like mine.

If she had one, why not the others?

Jenny looked at Tom. Handsome Tom, headstrong and a little arrogant, as even Jenny had to admit, if only to herself. What was he drawing now?

"Mine needs green, too. And yellow," he said.

"Mine needs black," said Dee and chuckled.

"All right, done," Audrey said.

"Come on, Jenny," Tom said. "Aren't you finished yet?"

Jenny looked down at her paper. She had made a formless doodle around the edges; the middle was blank. After an embarrassed moment with everyone's eyes on her, she turned the paper over and gave it to Dee. She would just have to explain later.

Dee shuffled all the slips and put them facedown in various rooms on the upper floors. "Now we put our paper dolls in the parlor downstairs," she said. "That's where we all start. And there should be a pile of game cards in the box, Summer, to tell us what to do and where to move. Put them in a stack on the table."

Summer did while Audrey fixed the paper dolls on

their little plastic anchors and set them up in the parlor.

"We need just one more thing," Dee said. She paused dramatically and then said, "The Shadow Man."

"Here he is," Summer said, picking up the last sheet of stiff tagboard from the box. "I'll cut out his friends first—the Creeper and the Lurker." She did, then handed the figures to Audrey. The Creeper was a giant snake, the Lurker a bristling wolf. Their names were printed in blood-red calligraphy.

"Charming," Audrey said, snapping anchors on. "Anywhere in particular I'm supposed to put them, Dee?"

"No, the cards will tell us when we meet them."

"Here's the Shadow Man. He can shadow me if he wants; I think he's cute," Summer said. Audrey took the paper doll from her, but as she did Jenny grabbed her wrist. Jenny couldn't speak. She couldn't breathe, actually.

It couldn't be—but it was. There was no question about it. The printed face that stared up at her was unmistakable.

It was the boy in black, the boy from the game store. The boy with the shocking blue eyes.

4

Jenny felt as if a black riptide was trying to suck her underwater. It was him. The boy from the game store. Every detail of his face was reproduced perfectly, but it wasn't a photograph. It was a drawing, like the snake and the wolf. The boy's hair was colored silvery-white with blue shadows. The artist had even captured his dark eyelashes. The portrait was so lifelike it looked as if those eyes might blink at any minute, as if the lips might speak.

And it *radiated* menace. Danger.

"What's the matter?" Audrey was saying. Her face swam in and out of focus as Jenny looked up. Jenny's eyes fixed on the beauty mark just above Audrey's upper lip. Audrey's lips were moving, but it was a minute before Jenny could make sense of the words. "What's wrong, Jenny?"

What could Jenny say?

I know this guy. I saw him at the store. He's a real

person, not some made-up character in a game. So . . .

So what? That's what they would ask her. What difference did it make? So the game must have been invented by somebody who knew the guy, and the guy had modeled for the picture. That would explain why the box was blank: Maybe it wasn't even a real, mass-produced game at all.

Or maybe the guy was crazy, had a fixation with this particular game, and had bleached his hair and dressed up to look like the game character. Dungeons and Dragons, Jenny thought suddenly—people were supposed to get heavily into that, sometimes even go overboard. That's the answer.

At least, it was the answer somebody here tonight would give. Tom, maybe, because Jenny could tell he wanted to play, and once Tom made up his mind on anything, he was immovable. Dee, because danger always kicked her. Zach, because the game involved art; or Summer, because she thought it was "cute." They all wanted to play.

A good hostess didn't get hysterical and ruin a party because she had shadows on the brain.

Jenny forced a smile.

"Nothing," she said, letting go of Audrey's wrist. "Sorry. I thought I recognized that picture. Silly, huh?"

"You been drinking the cough syrup again?" Michael inquired from the other side of the table.

"Are you all right, Thorny? Really?" Tom asked seriously. His green-flecked eyes searched hers, and Jenny felt her smile become more stable. She nodded. "Fine," she said firmly.

Tom got up and dimmed the track lighting.

"Hey," said Michael.

"We need it dark," Dee told them, "for this next part. The reading of the oath." She cut a glance at them, the whites of her eyes shining like smoky pearls.

"What oath?" Michael said warily.

"The Oath of the Game," Tom said. His voice was sinister. "It says here that we each have to swear that we're playing this game of our own free will, and that the game is real." Tom turned the lid of the box around for them to see. On the inside cover, above the printed instructions, was a large symbol. It was like a squared-off and inverted *U,* the two uneven horns of the letter pointing downward. It was deeply impressed in the cover and colored—as well as Jenny could tell in the dim light—rusty red.

I will not ruin this party, I will not ruin this party, Jenny thought. I *will not.*

Tom was reading from the instructions: " 'There is a Shadow World, like our own but different, existing alongside ours but never touching. Some people call it the world of dreams, but it is as real as anything else' . . . and then it says that entering the Shadow World can be dangerous, so you play at your own risk." He grinned around the group. "Actually, it says that the game can be hazardous to your life. You have to swear you understand that."

"I don't know if I like this anymore," Summer said.

"Come on," said Dee. "Live dangerously. Make it happen."

"Well . . ." Summer was taking this seriously. She pushed soft light curls off her forehead and frowned. "Is it getting warm in here?"

"Oh, swear, already," said Michael. "Let's get this thing over with. I swear I understand that this game may kill me before I'm old enough to get a McJob like my brother Dave."

"Now you." Dee stretched out a black-spandex-covered leg to nudge Zachary. "Swear."

"I swear," Zach said in bored tones, his thin face unreadable, his gray eyes cool as ever.

Summer sighed, capitulating. "Me, too, then."

Audrey adjusted her houndstooth jacket. "Me, three," she said. "And what about *you,* Deirdre?"

"I was just about to, Aud. I swear to have a great time and kick the Shadow Dude's ass."

Tom had gotten up and was lurking over Jenny. "How about it, devil woman? I swear—do you?"

Normally Jenny would have jabbed an elbow upward into his ribs. At the moment all she could manage was a colorless smile. They all wanted to do it. She was the hostess. They were her guests.

Tom wanted it.

"I swear," she said and was embarrassed when her voice cracked.

Tom cheered and tossed the box lid in the air. Dee's foot flashed out, kicking it back toward him. It fell on the floor by Jenny.

You jerk, if you really cared about me, you'd care about how *I* felt, Jenny thought in a rare moment of anger toward Tom. Then she squelched the thought. It was his birthday. He deserved to be indulged.

Something about the box lid caught her eye. For just an instant the upside-down *U* looked as if it were printed in red foil. It had—flashed—Jenny thought. But of course it couldn't have.

Everyone was kneeling around the table.

"Okay," said Dee. "All the little dollies in the parlor? Then somebody's got to turn a card. Who wants to be first?"

Jenny, feeling that if she was going to do this she might as well do it thoroughly, reached out and took the top card. It was glossy white like the game box and felt slick between her fingers. She turned it over and read: "'You have gathered with your friends in this room to begin the Game.'"

There was a pause. Then Summer giggled.

"Sort of an anticlimax," Audrey murmured. "Who's next?"

"Me," said Tom. He leaned over Jenny and took a card. He read, "'Each of you has a secret you would rather die than reveal.'"

Jenny stirred uneasily. It was just coincidence, because these were preprinted cards. But it did sound almost as if someone were answering the question she'd thought of earlier.

"My turn," Summer said eagerly. She read, "'You hear the sound of footsteps from one of the rooms above.'" She frowned. "But there aren't any rooms above. This is a one-story house."

Tom chuckled. "You're forgetting yourself. We're not *in* this house. We're in *that* house."

Summer blinked, her large blue eyes traveling over the pastel, basket-adorned walls of the Thornton living room. Then she looked at the Victorian paper house, with the seven paper dolls neatly arranged in the parlor like a group of guests too polite to go home. "Oh!"

She was just putting the card back when they all heard the noise from above.

Footsteps.

A quick light patter, like a child running on a wooden floor.

Summer shrieked and looked in terror at the ceiling.

Dee jumped up, her dark eyes blazing. Audrey stiffened. Michael grabbed at her, and she smacked his hand away. Zach's face was turned up; even his ponytail seemed to be tense. But Tom burst into laughter.

"It's squirrels," he got out finally. "They run on the roof all the time, don't they, Jenny?"

Jenny's stomach was knotted. Her voice wavered slightly as she said, "Yes, but—"

"But nothing. Somebody else take a card," Tom said. Nobody did. "All right, I'll do it myself. This is for you, Mike." He flipped a card.

"'You go to the door to get some air, but it seems to be stuck,'" he read. He looked around at the group. "Oh, come on. It's a *game*. Here, look." He stood up in a fluid motion and went to the sliding glass door that looked out on Jenny's backyard. Jenny saw his fingers moving, flipping the locks on the handle. A sense of dread overwhelmed her.

"Tom, don't!" she said. Before she knew what she was doing, she jumped up and took his arm. If he didn't try the door—if he didn't *try* it—the card couldn't come true.

Tom was jerking at the handle, ignoring her. "There's something wrong with it—there must be another lock."

"It's stuck," Michael said. He ran a hand through his rumpled **dark** hair, an oddly helpless gesture.

"Don't be stupid," Audrey snapped.

Dee's sloe eyes were glittering. Her hand darted

out and she took a card. "'None of the doors or windows in this house will open,'" she read.

Tom went on yanking furiously at the door. It wouldn't budge. Jenny caught his arm again. She was trembling all over with a sense of danger.

"Take another card," Zach said softly. There was something strange about his thin face—it was almost trancelike. Zombied out.

"No!" Jenny said.

Zachary was taking the card himself.

"No," said Jenny again. She had to stop this, but she couldn't let go of Tom. "Zach, don't read it."

"'You hear a clock strike nine,'" Zachary read softly.

"Jenny doesn't have any clocks that strike," Audrey said. She looked at Jenny sharply. "Do you? *Do you?"*

Jenny shook her head, her throat clogged. Every inch of her skin seemed to be raw, waiting. Listening.

Clear and sweet, the chimes rang out. The chimes of the clock at the game store, the clock she couldn't see. It seemed to be coming from far above. It began to strike the hour.

One. Two. Three. Four.

"Oh, God," Audrey said.

Five. Six. Seven.

At nine, Jenny thought. See you later—at nine.

Eight . . .

"Tom," Jenny whispered. The muscles in his arm were hard under her hand. Now, too late, he turned toward her.

Nine.

Then the wind came.

* * *
43

At first Jenny thought the riptide had gotten her. Then she thought it must be an earthquake. But all the time she had the sensation of air rushing by her, as if a hurricane had come in through the closed sliding glass door. A black, roaring hurricane that burned even as it froze. It hurt her like a physical thing, shaking her body and blinding her. She lost track of the room. The only thing real was the fistful of Tom's shirt she held.

Finally she lost track of that, too. The pain stopped for a while, and she just drifted.

She woke up on the floor.

It was like the only other time she'd ever fainted, when she and Joey had both been home sick with the flu. She'd jumped out of bed suddenly to tell him to turn down that stupid cartoon—and the next thing she knew she was waking up with her head in a wastebasket. Lying on the carpeted floor of her room, then, she had known that time had passed, without being sure how she knew it. This was the same.

Painfully Jenny lifted her head and blinked to bring the far wall into focus.

It didn't work. Something was wrong. The wall itself, which should have been pastel-colored and hung with weavings and baskets, was wrong. It was paneled with some dark wood, and an Oriental screen stood in front of it. Heavy velvet curtains obscured a window. A brass candlestick was attached to the wall. Jenny had never seen any of the things before.

Where am I?

The oldest question in the book, the biggest cliché.

But she really didn't know. She didn't know where she was or how she had gotten there, but she knew that whatever was going on was all wrong. Was—beyond her experience.

Things like this didn't happen.

It had happened anyway.

The two ideas jostled in her mind. She was already disoriented, on the verge of panic. Now she began to shake, and she felt a swelling in her throat.

No. Start screaming now and you'll never stop, she told herself. Don't think about it. You don't have to deal with it. Just find Tom.

Tom. For the first time Jenny looked at the floor. They were all lying there, Zach with his blond ponytail streaming out behind him (on a moss-green carpet worked with cabbage roses, but don't think about that, don't think about that now), Summer with her light curls cradled protectively in her small arms, Audrey with her French twist coming loose. Dee's long legs were sprawled near the window, and Michael's stocky body was curled in a ball beside her. Tom was lying against the wall—where the sliding glass door should have been. As Jenny got up unsteadily and began moving toward him, he stirred.

"Tom? Are you okay?" She took his hand, and when his warm, strong fingers closed around hers, she felt better. He groaned and opened his eyes.

"Hell of a headache," he muttered. "What happened?"

"I don't know," Jenny said in a small, precise voice. She was still close to having hysterics. She hung on to his hand hard enough to bruise. "We're not in the living room anymore."

It was just the truth, and she had to say it. She needed to share it with someone, the way Summer had needed to share about her dog being put to sleep. But Tom scowled.

"Don't be stupid," he said, and Jenny felt the little needle stab she always did when he snapped at her. "We can't be anywhere else. Everything's fine."

All his good humor had vanished, along with the rakish charm of his smile. His neat brown hair was just slightly mussed, and his green-flecked eyes looked both dazed and angry.

He's defensive, Jenny realized. Scared that it's his fault. She tried to squeeze his hand, but he was getting up.

So were the others. Dee was rubbing the back of her neck, looking around with quick, alert movements. She reached down and pulled a groaning Michael to his feet. Audrey was standing, too, her hands automatically going to fix the combs in her auburn hair even as she stared at the room.

Summer was cowering by the spindly-legged table that had taken the place of Jenny's mother's coffee table. Only Zach didn't seem frightened. He was standing and his clear gray eyes were open, but his lips moved soundlessly and he looked—entranced. As if he were moving in a dream.

Nobody said a word. They all looked around stupidly, trying to make sense of their surroundings.

They were standing in a Victorian parlor, lushly carpeted, furnished with Gothic Revival tables and chairs. A green lamp with a silk fringe hung from the ceiling. It looked like the perfect place for a seance.

Jenny *recognized* it.

She'd seen the pattern of the cabbage-rose carpet printed on tagboard. Zach had cut out the paneling with an X-Acto knife, and Audrey had put together that mahogany table.

They were in the paper house. It had come alive around them. They were *inside* it. . . .

Jenny's hands came slowly up to cover her mouth. Her heart had begun a deep, sick pounding.

"Oh, my God," Summer whispered. Then, with gathering force, "Oh, my God, oh, my *God*—"

Michael began to giggle hysterically.

"Shut up," Audrey said, breathing hard. "Both of you, shut up!"

Dee went to the wall and touched a candlestick, fingers dark against the bright brass. Then she reached up and stuck her fingers in the candle flame.

"Dee!" Tom rapped out.

"It's real," Dee said, looking at her fingertips. "It burns."

"Of course it's not real!" Audrey said. "This is all—some kind of illusion. Like virtual reality—"

Dee's eyes flashed. "It is *not* virtual reality. My mom's a computer expert—she knows what real VR is. Not the Pac-Man kind you get with video games. Even they can't do anything like this. Besides, where's the computer? Where's our helmets?" She smacked a flattened hand against the wall. "No, this is *real.*"

Michael was feeling a chair, still half giggling. "So maybe it was some of Audrey's mushrooms. What were they called? Shiitake? Maybe it's a judgment on us."

"Take it easy, Mike," Tom said. He looked angry,

which Jenny knew meant he was feeling uncertain. She watched him, all the while stroking the smooth mahogany of a tabletop. She felt the same compulsion that Dee and Michael obviously did—to *touch* things here. She kept expecting them to feel like cardboard, but they were real.

"Okay," Tom said, "we're *not* in the living room. We've been—moved somehow. Somebody's playing a joke on us. But we don't have to just stand around like idiots and take it."

"What do you suggest we do?" Audrey said acidly.

Tom strode over to the parlor doorway, which opened on a dim hall. "The guys can come with me and scout around; you girls stay here and keep your eyes open."

Dee threw him a scornful look, then turned narrowed eyes on "the guys." Michael was tapping on the walls, muttering, and Zach was just staring, the skin of his face drawn tight over bones. Jenny wanted to go to him, but she couldn't move.

"Good luck," Dee said to Tom. "Hurry back to protect us."

"Don't anybody leave," Summer said, her blue eyes wet.

"You protect *Jenny,*" Tom snarled at Dee, thrusting his face close to hers. Jenny felt an instant of throbbing warmth, which was immediately swept away by coldness. How could anyone protect anyone here?

Dee crossed the room and put an arm, hard as a boy's, around Jenny's shoulders. "Right," she said.

"I think we should stay together," Michael said nervously.

"Oh, what's the *difference?*" Audrey said. "It's not really happening anyway. We're not here."

"Then what is it?" Summer asked, on the verge of hysteria. "Where are we?"

"In the Game."

The voice came from the corner of the room, from the shadow behind the Oriental screen. It was a voice that didn't belong to any of the group, but one that was familiar to Jenny. She'd only heard it once before, but she couldn't mistake it. Like water over rock, it was full of elemental music.

Every head turned.

The boy stepped out of the shadows.

He was just as beautiful as he had been in the store. But here, against the backdrop of this quaint and fussy room, he looked even more exotic. His hair shone in the dimness like white cat's fur or mountain snow. He was wearing a black vest that showed the smooth, hard muscles of his bare arms, and pants that looked like snakeskin. His eyes were heavy-lidded, shielded by long lashes. He was smiling.

Summer gasped. "The picture. The paper doll in the box. It's *him*—"

"The Shadow Man," Michael said hoarsely.

"Don't make me laugh," Tom said. Lip curled, he looked the apparition up and down. "Who the hell are you? What do you want?"

The boy in black took another step forward. Jenny could see the impossible daylight color of his eyes now, though he wasn't looking at her. His gaze swept over the others, and Jenny could see it affect them, like a wave of cold air that caused them to draw together. She could see each of them reacting as they

49

looked into his face and saw—something there. Something that caused their eyes to go wide and suspicion to turn to fear.

"Why don't you call me Julian?"

"Is that your name?" Tom said, much more quietly.

"It's as good as anything else."

"Whoever you are, we're not scared of you," Dee said suddenly, letting go of Jenny and stepping forward. It sounded like the truth, as if Dee, anyway, was not afraid, and it seemed to encourage the others.

"We want to know what's going on," Tom said, loudly again.

"We haven't done anything to you. Please just let us go home," Summer added.

"You can't go home again," Zach murmured. It was the first time he'd spoken. He was wearing a strange half smile.

"Bud, you're in worse shape than I am," Michael told him in a low voice. Zach didn't answer.

Only Jenny stayed back, not moving, not speaking. Her sense of dread was getting stronger all the time. She was remembering a look like a starving tiger's.

"At least tell us what we're doing here," Audrey said.

"Playing the Game."

They all stared at him.

"You agreed to play. You read the rules."

"But—playing? What playing? You mean—"

"Don't talk to him about it, Mike," Tom interrupted. "We're not going to play his stupid game."

He's so scared, Jenny thought. He still thinks this is all his fault. But it isn't, Tom, it isn't. . . .

"I mean," the boy in black said to Michael, "that you all swore you were playing of your own free will and that you knew the Game was real. You invoked the rune Uruz." He sketched a shape in the air with his finger, an inverted *U*. Jenny noticed that the snake tattoo she'd seen on his wrist in the store had vanished. "You pierced the veil between the worlds."

Audrey laughed, a sharp false sound like glass shattering.

Michael breathed, "This is nuts."

Dee's expression said that she agreed. "What's a *rune?*"

Audrey opened her mouth, then shut it again tightly, shaking her head. Julian's lip quirked and he lowered his voice.

"It's magic," he said. "A mystical letter from an ancient alphabet. In this case designed to let you walk between the worlds. If you don't understand it, you shouldn't be messing with it."

"We didn't mean to mess with anything," Summer whispered. "It's all a mistake."

The fear in the room had heightened. Jenny could sense it like a yellow aura enveloping them all.

"No mistake. You chose to play the Game," the boy said again. "Now you play until you win—or I do."

"But *why?*" Summer said, almost sobbing. "What do you want from us?"

Julian smiled, then looked past her. Past all of them, to the one person who hadn't said a word since he'd entered the room. To Jenny.

"Every game has a prize," he said.

Jenny met the impossibly blue eyes and knew she'd been right.

They stood for a moment, looking at each other.

Julian's smile deepened. Tom looked back and forth between them. Understanding slowly dawned on his face.

"No . . ." he whispered.

"Every game has a prize," the boy repeated. "Winner take all."

"No!" Tom said and launched himself across the room.

5

Tom lunged at the boy in black—and drew up short. His eyes were fixed on something at his feet. Jenny couldn't understand it—it was as if he saw something terrifying there on the carpet. He turned to get away from it and stopped. It was behind him, too. Slowly he backed up against the wall.

Jenny was staring at him in dismay. It was like watching one of the mimes out at Venice Beach. A very good mime—Jenny could tell that the things Tom was facing were small, that they were trying to climb up his legs, and that he was terribly afraid of them. But there was nothing on the carpet.

"Tom," she said in a thin voice and took a step.

"Don't come near me! They'll get you, too!"

It was awful. Tom, who was never afraid of anything, was cornered by empty air. His lips were drawn back from his teeth, his chest was heaving.

"What is it?" Summer whimpered.

The others were all staring in silence. Jenny

whirled on the boy in black, who was leaning against the parlor wall and watching in amusement.

"What are you doing to him?"

"In the Game you have to face your nightmares. This is just a free sample of Tom's. No reason for the rest of you to be in on it."

Jenny faced Tom, drawing a deep breath. She took a step toward him.

"Stay back!" Tom said, sharp and frightened.

"Doesn't look like he's conquered it yet," Julian remarked.

Jenny stepped right into the midst of what Tom was staring at. She felt nothing but air around her bare ankles. She saw nothing. But Tom did—he yanked her to him, to the wall, falling down with her to his knees. He kicked out.

"Tom, don't! There's nothing there! Tom, *look* at me!"

His green-flecked eyes were wild. "Keep away from her. Keep back!" He was scuffing with his outstretched foot at the empty floor beside Jenny, trying to push something away. His mouth was quivering with disgust.

"Tom," she sobbed, shaking him. He didn't even glance at her. She buried her face in his shoulder, holding him with all her strength. Trying to will him sane again.

And then—her arms collapsed in on themselves. It was like one of those magician's tricks where the beautiful girl is hidden beneath a sheet—and then the sheet caves in and falls to the floor. Tom was there—Tom wasn't there. Like that. Jenny's embracing arms were empty.

She screamed.

And looked helplessly, wildly down at her hands, at her lap. At the floor. Tom couldn't be gone.

He was.

She looked behind her and saw that the others were, too.

Jenny's eyes darted to the dim hallway. It was empty. The curtains over the window were flat and still. But Dee was gone, and Audrey was gone, and Zach and Michael and Summer were all gone from the parlor. All five of them, without a sound. The way things vanish in dreams.

Please let it be a dream, Jenny thought. I've had enough, now. Please, I'm sorry; let it be a dream.

She was clutching the carpet so tensely that her fingernails were bending back. It hurt, and the pain didn't wake her up. Nothing changed. Her friends were still gone.

The boy in black was still there.

"Where did they go? What did you do with them?" she said. She was so dazed that it came out as a sort of insane calm.

Julian smiled whimsically. "They're upstairs, scattered around the house, waiting to face their nightmares. Waiting for you. You'll find them as you go through the Game."

"As *I* go?" Jenny said stupidly. "Look, you don't understand. I don't know what's—"

"You're the main player here, you know," he interrupted, gently chiding. "The door back to your world is at the top of the house, and it's open. If you can get to it, you can go. Bring your friends and they can leave, too."

Jenny's mind was still stuck on one thing. "Where's Tom? I want—"

"Your—Tom—is at the top." He pronounced the name as if it were something not mentioned in polite society. "I'll be giving him my *special* attention. You'll see him when you get there—if you get there."

"Look, please. I don't want to play any game." Jenny was still speaking as if this was all a mistake that would be cleared up somehow, as long as she stayed rational. As long as she avoided his eyes. "I don't know what you're thinking, but—"

He interrupted again. "And if you *don't* get there, then I win. And you stay here, with me."

"What do you mean—with you?" Jenny said sharply, jerked out of her courtesy.

He smiled. "I mean that you stay in this place, in my world. With me—as mine."

Jenny stared at him—and then she was on her feet, her composure shattering. "You're out of your mind!" she said. She would have lunged at him, herself, if she'd ever had any practice at violence.

"Careful, Jenny."

She stopped, frightened by what she sensed in him. Looking into his eyes, she saw something so alien, so terrifying, that she couldn't move. It was then, at last, that she *believed* what was happening. Full realization of what this boy had done, of everything that had happened tonight, crashed in on her. The young man standing before her, looking almost human, could do magic.

"Oh, God," she whispered.

All her violence had drained away, replaced by a fear older and deeper than anything she'd ever experienced. An old, old recognition. Something inside her knew him from a time when girls took skin bags to the river to get water, a time when panthers walked in the darkness outside mud huts. From a time before electric lights, before candles, when darkness was fended off with stone lamps. When darkness was the greatest danger of all.

Jenny looked at the boy standing beside her with his hair shining like moonlight. If Darkness had taken on a face and a voice, if the powers of night had gathered themselves together and formed themselves into a human being, they would have made something like this.

"Who are you?" whispered Jenny.

"Don't you know yet?"

Jenny shook her head.

"Never mind. You will, before the Game is over."

Jenny tried to regain her calm. "Look—let's just . . . You were at the game store."

"I was waiting for you."

"So this was all—set up? But why *me?* Why are you doing this to *me?*" Jenny could feel hysteria tugging at her again.

Then he said it. He was looking at her with eyes like the sky on a November morning, one corner of his mouth turned up. He spoke gravely and a little formally.

"Because," he said, "I've fallen in love with you."

Jenny stared at him.

"Surprised? You shouldn't be. I first saw you a long time ago—you were such a pretty little girl. As if there was sunshine all around you. Do you know the story of Hades?"

"What?" She didn't like this mercurial jumping from subject to subject.

"Hades," he said encouragingly, like someone helping her cram for a final. "Greek god of the Underworld. Ruler there. He lived in the world of shadows—and he was lonely. And then one day he looked up to the earth's surface and saw Persephone. Picking wildflowers, I think. Laughing. He fell in love with her on the spot. He wanted to make her his queen, but he knew perfectly well she wouldn't go with him willingly. So . . ."

"So?" Jenny got out.

"So he hitched his black horses to his chariot. And the earth split open in front of Persephone's feet. And her wildflowers fell to the ground."

"That's a story," Jenny said, trying to keep her voice steady. "A myth. There's no such person as Hades."

"Are you sure?" After a moment Julian went on: "Anyway, you're luckier than Persephone, Jenny. You have a chance to get away. I could just take you, but I'm giving you a chance." He looked at Jenny with eyes like liquid sapphires, wild exotic eyes. She couldn't speak, couldn't look away.

"Who are you?" she whispered again.

"Who do you want me to be? I love you, Jenny—I came from the World of Shadows to get you. I'll be anything you like, give you anything you want. Do you like jewels? Emeralds to match your eyes? Diamonds?" He reached outspread fingers toward her throat, not quite touching.

"What about clothes? A different outfit for every hour of the day, in colors you've never imagined.

Pets? Have a marmoset, or a white tiger. Far-off places? You can lie in the sun at Cabo San Lucas or Côte d'Azur. Anything, Jenny. Just imagine."

Jenny covered her face with her hands. "You're *crazy.*"

"I can make your wildest dreams come true. Literally. Ask me for something, something you thought you could never have. Quick; I may not make the offer again."

Jenny was almost sobbing. His voice, soft and insistent, made her feel as if she were falling. She had a terrifying desire to collapse in his arms.

"*Now,* Jenny, while we're still friends. Later, things won't be so pleasant. I don't want to hurt you, but I will if it's necessary. Save yourself a lot of pain and bother and let me make you happy now. Give in, yield to me. It's going to happen eventually, anyway."

The sensation of falling vanished. Jenny's head snapped up. "Oh, really?"

"I never lose."

Something was waking up in Jenny. Usually she got angry quickly and got over it as quickly, like a summer cloudburst. Now she felt the slow kindling of something different, a deliberate, steady fury that would burn a long time.

"Careful, Jenny," Julian said again softly.

"I will never give in to you," Jenny told him, equally soft. "I'll die first."

"It won't come to that, I hope. But other things might happen—once you start playing the Game, I can't change the rules. Your friends might suffer."

"What? How?"

He shook his head at her. "Jenny, Jenny. Don't you understand anything that's going on? They're all playing the Game. They agreed to take the risks. Now they'll have to take the consequences." He turned.

"No—wait!"

"It's too late, Jenny. I gave you a chance; you refused it. From now on we'll be playing the Game."

"But—"

"You can start with this riddle." Turning back, head tilted slightly, he recited:

"I am just two and two. I am hot. I am cold.
I'm the parent of numbers that cannot be told.
I'm a gift beyond measure, a matter of course,
And I'm yielded with pleasure—when taken by
    force."

Jenny shook her head. "That tells who *you* are?"

He laughed. "No, that tells what I want from you. Give me the answer, and I'll let one of your friends go."

Jenny pushed the riddle to the back of her mind. It didn't make any sense, and while Julian was in the room, it was impossible to concentrate on anything else but him.

In all this time he hadn't lost his whimsical good cheer, his charm. He was obviously loving this game, having a wonderful time.

"That's all," he said. "Let the Game begin. By the way, if you get hurt in these nightmares, you get hurt for real. If you die, you die. And I can tell you right off that one of you probably won't make it."

60

Jenny's head jerked up. "Who?"

"That would be telling. Let's just say that one of you probably doesn't have the strength to get through. Oh, and did I mention the time limit? The door in the turret—the door back to your own world—is going to close at dawn. Which tomorrow is at exactly six-eleven. If you can't get to it by then, you're stuck here—so don't waste your time. Here's something to remind you."

Far away but clear, an unseen clock chimed. Jenny turned toward the sound, counting unconsciously as it struck. Ten.

When she turned back, Julian was gone.

Jenny held herself motionless. There was no sound. The fringe on the green velvet lamp rippled slightly; otherwise the room was still.

For an instant just being alone was enough to panic her. She was by herself in a house that didn't exist.

No, don't freak. *Think.* You can look around now. Maybe there's a way out of here.

She went to the window, pulled the heavy peacock-blue curtain aside. Then she froze.

At first she simply stared, breath catching in her throat, feeling her eyes go wide like a deer's. Then she whipped the curtain back in place, jerking it past the closing point, pressing it against the window with her hands. She could hardly make herself let go of the velvety material, but she did, and then she backed away quickly. She didn't want to see outside again.

A landscape of elemental terror. Like something out of the Ice Age—as painted by a mad impressionist. A blizzard with huge ungainly shapes lumbering through it. Blue and green flashes like lightning giving glimpses of deformed creatures crawling over icy ground. Twisted pinnacles of rock corkscrewing up toward a blank white sky.

She wouldn't survive a minute out there.

When the devil goes ice-skating, Jenny thought. So what if Hell's already frozen?

Oh, how funny. Michael would appreciate that. She felt tears sting her nose, her eyes. She stood hunched and miserable, hugging her own elbows in the center of the empty room. She had never felt so alone—or so frightened.

She missed her friends desperately. Dee's courage, Michael's humor, Audrey's practicality. Even Summer would give Jenny someone to protect, and as for Zach—she wanted to find out what was wrong with him. In all the years she'd known him, she'd never seen him act this way.

But most of all she wanted Tom.

Tom, she thought fiercely. *He's* the one in trouble. Not you. He's going through God knows what, getting Julian's *special* attention. And you have no business standing here moaning while that's happening.

The yelling at herself actually helped—it shut up the babbling little voices in the back of her mind telling her that she couldn't deal.

Julian had said it depended on her.

All right. She was calmer now. She knew she had to start moving—but *where?* Jenny tried to gather her scattered thoughts, to remember the configuration of the paper house. The parlor had been off a long central hallway on the first floor. At the end of that hallway there had been a staircase.

Upstairs, Julian had said.

Jenny found herself moving through the candle-lit hallway, past gold-framed portraits which looked down disapprovingly from the walls.

She looked up at the stairway.

It was wide, carpeted down the middle. There was absolutely nothing strange about it—and Jenny couldn't force herself to put a foot on it.

I could turn around and run, she thought. It was impossible to realize—*emotionally*—that she couldn't just go back into the parlor and find a way home.

But intellectually she knew there was nothing in the parlor to help her. And she didn't want to think what she might see if she opened the front door of this house.

So you can stay here and hide, or you can go up. You have to choose.

She put a foot on the stairway. It was solid. Like any stairway. She started climbing toward the darkness at the top.

The hallway on the second floor seemed to stretch on forever in both directions, so dark that Jenny couldn't see any end to it. There were candles in brass candle holders at intervals on the walls, but they were far apart and didn't give much light. Jenny didn't remember any hall in the paper house looking this way. In fact, what this place *really* looked like was the Haunted Mansion at Disneyland. Like every other kid in southern California, Jenny had been to Disneyland so often she knew

63

it by heart, and she recognized the creepy wall-paper.

But that was ridiculous. Why should it look like that?

She walked with fingertips brushing the wall. A dozen steps down the hall she saw something far ahead in the dimness, moving under the flickering light of a candle.

Jenny didn't know whether to run toward it or away. Then she noticed something familiar in the long legs and the greyhound build of the figure.

"Dee!"

Dee barely glanced up as Jenny reached her. She was wrestling with a door which bulged just like a door in the Haunted Mansion, the one that had always scared Jenny as a child. A lot of the things in the Haunted Mansion were simply silly, and a lot of others were mind-boggling—but only one thing there had ever really frightened Jenny when she was young . . . and that was a door.

A closed door, which bulged in the middle as if a great weight was leaning on it from the inside, deforming the wood, expanding, relaxing. While all the time guttural snarls, not the sort of sounds a human could make, came from behind it.

The door that Dee was wrestling with was doing exactly the same thing.

Only it was open a little. Dee had her lynxlike body braced against it, head down, knees bent, one long slender leg back so the toe of her sneaker dug into the black carpet of the hallway, but she couldn't quite get the door shut.

Without a word Jenny went and helped her, leaning to press on the door above and below the handle which Dee was grasping. The keyhole had a large key in it.

"Push," Dee gasped.

Jenny leaned harder, throwing her weight behind it, while Dee pushed right above her, body stretched taut beside Jenny's. The door pushed back and bulged. The low, thick snarling rose in tone. Angrily. Jenny felt her muscles begin to tremble. She put her head down and shut her eyes, teeth locking.

"Push!"

The door yielded a crucial fraction of an inch, closing. Dee's hand shot to the key and turned it. There was a click, the sound of a bolt shooting home.

The door wasn't pushing anymore.

Jenny stumbled back, legs weak with the sudden release of strain, and looked at it. No bulging. No snarling now, either. It was just an ordinary six-paneled door, as quiet and innocent as a door could be.

There was utter silence in the hallway.

Jenny backed to the opposite wall, then slowly slid down it until she was resting on her heels. Her forehead was wet around her hair roots.

Dee was leaning one hand against the wall by the door.

"Hi," Jenny said at last.

"Hi."

They continued to look at each other blankly.

"Have you seen the others?"

Dee shook her head.

"Me, either. He said—you know, *him*"—Jenny

paused until Dee nodded—"he said you guys were scattered around the house. Waiting for your nightmares." Jenny looked at the door. "Were you in there?"

"No. I was in the parlor watching Tom, and then all of a sudden I got dizzy. I woke up on the floor here. There was only one door, and I wondered what was inside, so I opened it."

"Oh. What *was* inside?"

"Just your average butt-ugly monster."

"Like the ones in the pictures—the Creeper and the Lurker or whatever?"

"No, *really* ugly. Sort of like Coach Rogers."

Dee was taking this rather calmly, Jenny thought. She looked strained and stern, but very beautiful, like a statue carved out of ebony.

"We'd better look around," she said. "See if we can find the others."

"Okay." Jenny didn't move.

Dee, still standing, reached out to her.

"Come on. Up."

"I'm going to faint."

"Don't you *dare*. On your feet, soldier!"

Jenny got up. She looked down the hallway. "I thought you said there was only one door. What's that, then?"

"It wasn't there before."

They both looked at the door. It was just like the other one, six-paneled, innocuous.

"What do you think is behind this one?" Jenny said carefully.

"Let's see." Dee reached for the knob.

"Wait, you lunatic!" Trying not to flinch, Jenny pressed her ear to the wood. She couldn't hear anything but her own breathing. "Okay—but be ready to shut it again fast."

Dee flashed her a barbaric grin and stood ready to kick the door shut. Jenny put her hand on the knob, turned it.

"Now," Dee said, and Jenny flung the door open.

6

The room behind the door had golden-ocher walls. On one of them an African mask hung in primitive glory. Several clay sculptures rested on built-in teak shelving, including a bust that could have been Nefertiti. Leather cushions were tossed around the floor, one resting beside a complete home gym.

It was Dee's bedroom. The bust was one that Dee's grandmother, Aba, had made of Dee. There was a stack of textbooks by the bed and a pile of half-completed homework on the nightstand.

Jenny loved this room, loved to see what Aba would bring Dee next from her travels. But seeing it now was unnerving.

Once they were inside, the door shut behind them—and disappeared. When Jenny turned at the sound of slamming, she saw nothing but a blank ocher wall where the door used to be.

"Great—now we're trapped," Jenny said.

Dee was frowning. "There must be a way out."

They tried the window. Instead of the Ice Age outside it was the ordinary view from Dee's upstairs room. Jenny could see the grass below, illuminated by a porch light. But the window wouldn't budge, or—as they discovered when Dee swung a ten-pound barbell against it—break.

"So now what?" Jenny said. "Why are we in your room? I don't understand what's going *on.*"

"If this place is like a dream and we know we're dreaming it, we should be able to change things. With our minds. Maybe we're supposed to *make* a way out of here."

They both tried, with no results. No matter how hard Jenny concentrated on making the door re-appear, nothing happened.

"I give up." Dee took off her jacket and flopped on the bed—as if this place really were her room.

Jenny sat beside her, trying to think. Her brain wasn't working properly—shock, she supposed. "All right, look. That guy said we're each supposed to face our nightmares. So this must be—" she began, but Dee interrupted.

"What else did he say? Who is he?"

"Oh. Do you . . . do you believe in the devil?"

Dee gave her a scornful look. "The only devil I know is Dakaki, and he only makes you horny. According to Aba."

"I think he wanted me to believe he was the devil," Jenny said softly. "But I don't know."

"And he wants us to play the Game with him? Just like the one in the box, only for real?"

"If we get to the turret by dawn, we can go," Jenny said. "If we don't, he wins." She looked at the other girl. "Dee, aren't you scared?"

"Of the supernatural?" Dee shrugged. "What's to be scared of? I always liked sword-and-sorcery stuff; I'm glad it's true. And I don't see why we can't beat him. I swore to kick the Shadow Man's ass before—and I'm going to. You wait."

"But—this is all so crazy," Jenny said. Now that she had time to sit and think, reaction was setting in. She was shaking again. "It's like you've always thought, sure, maybe there's ESP, maybe there're strange things out there in the dark. But you never think it could happen to *you.*"

Dee opened her mouth, but Jenny rushed on.

"And then it does and everything's different and it isn't possible and *it's still happening.*" She looked hard into the dark eyes with the slightly amber-tinted whites, desperate for understanding.

"That's right," Dee said briefly, returning Jenny's gaze. "It *is* happening. So all the rules are changed. We have to adapt—fast. Or we're not going to make it."

"But—"

"But nothing, Jenny. You know what your problem is? You think too much. There's no point in talking about it anymore. What we have to worry about now is surviving."

Dee's straightforward, razor-sharp mind had gone to the heart of the matter. What was happening was happening, possible or not. They had to deal with it if they wanted to live. Jenny wanted to live.

"Right," she breathed. "So we adapt."

Dee flashed her brilliant smile. "Besides, it's kind of fun," she said. "Don't you think?"

Jenny thought of Tom cowering from something

invisible on the floor. She leaned her forehead onto her fingertips.

"Something must scare you, though," she said after a minute, looking up. "You drew a nightmare."

Dee picked up a beaded Ndebele bracelet from the nightstand and examined it. "My mom scares me. Really," she added, at Jenny's disgusted look. "Her stuff at the university—computers and all." Dee glanced toward the window.

Jenny saw only the curtains made of appliqué cloth from Dahomey.

"You're afraid of *technology?*" she said in disbelief.

"I am not afraid of technology. I just like to be able to deal with things—you know, directly." Dee held up a slender clenched fist, and Jenny looked at the corded tendons in the dark forearm. No wonder Dee wasn't afraid of the "sword and sorcery" stuff—she fit right into the heroic mythos.

"It's the same reason I won't go to college," Dee said. "I want to work with my hands. And not at anything arty."

"Aba would smack you," Jenny told her. "And your brain's as good as your hands—" She broke off because Dee was once again looking at the window.

"Dee, what did you draw?" she said, sitting up straight and finally asking the question she should have asked in the first place.

"Nothing's happening."

"What did you draw?"

A red light was blossoming outside the window, like the glow of a distant fire. Jenny whipped her head toward a crackling sound and saw that Dee's stereo had begun to smoke.

71

"What—?" Jenny breathed. Dee was already moving toward the window.

"What's going to happen?" Jenny yelled, jumping up. She had to yell because of the throbbing sound that suddenly permeated the room. It resonated in Jenny's bones.

Outside, a silhouette appeared against the light.

"Dee!" Jenny grabbed for the other girl, trying to pull her away from the window. She was panicking and she knew it. The thing outside was *huge,* blocking out the stars, dull black and nonreflective itself but haloed in its own red glow. The eucalyptus trees outside were thrashing in a violent wind.

"What is it?" Jenny screamed, dimly aware that Dee was clutching back at her. But that was a stupid question. What *could* it be, hovering outside a second-story window, shaped like a half-sphere with the flat side down? As Jenny watched, six beams of light, bright as phosphorous flares, shot out from the bottom of the thing.

One of the lights swung around to shine directly through the window. Jenny was blinded, but she heard the shivery tinkle of glass, and a blast of wind blew her hair straight back. The window's gone, she thought.

The wind roaring past her was freezing and felt somehow electric. Behind her a brass tray fell off a wooden stand with a crash.

That was when Jenny found she couldn't move. The light was paralyzing her somehow, her muscles going like jelly. There was the strong pungent odor of an electric storm.

She was losing consciousness.

I'm going to die, she thought. I'll never wake up.

With a great effort she turned her head toward Dee for help. Dee was facing the light stiffly, pupils contracted to pinpoints. Unable to help Jenny or herself.

Fight, Jenny thought weakly.

This time fainting was like oozing into a black puddle of sludge.

The room was round. Jenny was lying on a table that conformed to her body's shape. Her eyes were burning and tearing, and she felt a great disinclination to move. A white light shone down on her from above.

"It's exactly the way I thought it would be," a husky voice said. Jenny fought off the lassitude enough to turn her head. Dee was on another table a few feet away. "It's just like what I've read about the Visitors, just like my dreams."

Jenny had never thought much about UFOs at all, but this wasn't what she would have expected. The only thing she knew about aliens was that they—did things—to people.

"So this was your nightmare," she said.

Dee's perfect profile was tilted up toward the white spotlight above her, looking *exactly* like an Egyptian carving. "Oh, brilliant," she said. "Any other deductions?"

"Yes," said Jenny. "We've got to get out of here."

"Can't move," Dee said. "Can you?"

There were no obvious restraints, but Jenny's arms and legs were too heavy to lift. She could breathe and move her torso a little, but her limbs were dead weights.

I'm scared, Jenny thought. And then she thought

about how Dee must feel. As an athlete, physical helplessness was Dee's worst fear. The strong, slim body that she'd cultivated with so much care was no use at all to her now.

"This place—it's so sterile," Dee said, her nostrils flaring. "Smell it? And I bet they're like hive insects, all the same. If we could just get up to fight them . . . but they've got *weapons,* obviously."

Jenny understood. Muscle and ingenuity wouldn't do anything against sterile, hellishly efficient technology. No wonder it was Dee's personal nightmare.

Jenny noticed a movement in her peripheral vision.

They were small—Summer's size. To Jenny they looked like demons: hairless, with slender bodies and large glittering dark eyes. No noses, slits for mouths.

Their skin glowed like bad mushrooms—very pale mushrooms grown in a cellar without ever seeing the light. Jenny noticed an odor of almonds.

They were alive, but they were as alien and *wrong* as the bleached things that crawl around at the bottom of caves. Just the sight of them struck Jenny with sick terror.

They were naked, but Jenny couldn't see anything that would make them male or female. Their bodies were hideous blanks, like dolls' bodies. They're *its,* Jenny thought.

Somehow, Jenny knew they were going to hurt her.

Dee made a faint sound.

Jenny turned toward her. It was easier than it had been the other time, and after an instant she realized that the spotlight above her had dimmed fractionally. Dee's light was brighter, because Dee was trying to get away.

Jenny had never seen Dee frightened before—even in the parlor Dee had looked more alert than anything else. But now Dee looked like a terrified animal. Droplets of sweat stood on her forehead with the effort to move. The more she thrashed, the brighter the light above her got.

"Dee, stop it," Jenny said, agonized. She couldn't stand to watch. "It's just a dream, Dee! Don't let it get to you."

But Julian had said if they got hurt in the dream, they got hurt for real.

The Visitors were clustering around Dee, but they didn't seem alarmed. They seemed absolutely indifferent. One of them pushed a cart over to the far side of Dee's table. Jenny saw a tray of gleaming instruments.

God—no, Jenny thought.

Dee collapsed back on the table, exhausted.

Another being picked up something long and shiny from the tray, examined it with lustrous black eyes. It flexed the thing a few times like a painter making practice runs with a brush. It seemed dissatisfied, although with its masklike face Jenny didn't know how she could tell this. Then it casually flicked the thing up Dee's thigh and Dee screamed.

It was like hearing your father scream. Jenny was so frightened that she tried to get up, and only succeeded in disarranging her legs slightly. One of the beings repositioned them carefully, stretching her feet toward the bottom corners of the table.

She had never felt so open, so utterly vulnerable.

Dee's black spandex legging gaped where the thing had cut it. Jenny could see blood.

The being handed the instrument to one of the

others, which took it away. If they were talking or communicating, Jenny couldn't sense it. Certainly nobody tried to communicate with Dee or Jenny.

They were moving around again. One of them— the same one who had cut Dee?—took up a new instrument and went to Jenny's table. With a swift, deft movement the being touched the instrument to Jenny's hand. Jenny felt a pinch.

Then the probe went in her ear. Outraged, Jenny tried to roll her head away, but small hands—strong as claws inside mushroom flesh—held her forehead. She felt the probe go in deeper, and she squirmed frantically. It touched her eardrum and hurt like a Q-tip stabbed too deep.

She was completely helpless. Whatever they wanted to do to her, they would do.

Tears of pain and fury trickled out of her eyes, down her temples. They put the probe in her other ear. One of them dabbed at her eye, holding the lid open. Jenny felt the touch of cool metal against her eyeball.

"It's just a dream," she called to Dee, almost sobbing, when the probe was withdrawn. "It's not real!"

She couldn't hear any answer from the other table.

What kind of game was this, where you didn't have a chance? Julian had talked about "getting through" the nightmares, but Jenny didn't think that meant just waiting for them to pass. She was supposed to *do* something, but she didn't know what, and she couldn't move. And she didn't think she and Dee were going to survive this if they just lay here.

"What do you want from us?" she shouted. "What are we supposed to do?"

There was a shifting among the Visitors. A new kind of being had arrived. Taller than the others, clearly in command, with skin as white as wax. Its fingers were twice as long as a human's. Although Jenny got only a glimpse of its face, it looked more menacing than the other kind, its features even more exaggerated.

It picked something up from the instrument cart and went over to the far side of Dee's table. It looked up at Jenny, and she saw its eyes were blue.

Not glittering black like the other beings' eyes. Blue lakes endlessly deep, deep as a mountain is high. Eyes that looked *inside* you.

Jenny stared back, her own eyes widening.

Then she saw what it was holding. A needle. Wire-thin, murderously long, longer than the needle for a spinal tap. The tall Visitor was holding it over Dee's stomach.

Dee's stomach was heaving wildly in a fight for breath. Her khaki T-shirt was sticking to her body as she writhed in a futile attempt to escape. Her sweat-soaked hair glistened like mica in the light.

"Don't touch her!" Jenny cried. To watch it happen to Dee was worse than having it happen to herself.

The needle hovered just below Dee's navel. Dee's abdomen went concave trying to avoid it. Dee made rocking, shifting motions as if trying to shimmy up the table, but she only moved in place. The light above her intensified, and abruptly her struggles became weaker.

"You bastard! Leave her alone!"

What can I *do?* Jenny thought. She had to stop this—but how?

77

The light.

It came to her suddenly. The light above her had dimmed as Dee's had brightened. Maybe she could move now. And if she could move—

She began to rock.

She had some control over her body. Not much. Her arms and legs were still useless, like huge pieces of dead meat attached to her. But she could move her trunk and her head and neck. Using all her strength, she rocked her weight from one side to the other.

Dee saw her. All the other eyes in the room, all those slanted liquidy black eyes, and the one pair of deep blue, were on Dee's stomach, on the needle. But Dee's thrashing head had turned toward Jenny, and just for a moment the two of them were looking at each other, communicating without words. Then Dee began to struggle again.

The harder Dee fought, the brighter the light over Dee. The brighter the light over Dee, the dimmer the light over Jenny.

Fall off this table and you'll have no way to control it, Jenny's mind told her. A broken arm or leg, at least, and maybe a broken nose. You'll smash into the floor facedown.

She kept on rocking. Maybe Dee thought she was just trying to get away, but what Jenny cared about was distracting them. Stopping that *thing* with its too-long fingers from putting the needle in Dee. If she hurt herself they'd have to come deal with her. They'd leave Dee alone.

She swung her torso harder and harder, like a beetle trying to upend itself. Dee was fighting madly, yelling out insults to keep the aliens' attention. The light above Jenny dimmed further, Jenny surged violently—and felt her momentum take her over the edge. For a moment she teetered there, balanced on her side, then the deadweight of her arms and legs decided the issue, and she felt herself begin to fall.

There was a burst of startled movement from the aliens, and the light flamed into brightness above her. It didn't matter in the least. It wasn't her muscles that were in charge, it was the law of gravity. Something nobody could argue with.

Jenny thought.

Searing illumination was reflecting off the white floor, and Jenny shut her eyes as that floor seemed to come up to meet her. She flinched away from the moment of impact. When the impact didn't come, she opened her eyes.

She was floating, facedown, an inch or so from the floor. Suspended. Paralyzed. The aliens were scuttling around hysterically, as if they weren't programmed to deal with this. As if they were as surprised by her midair arrest as she was.

The painful reflection on the floor softened. Jenny was still floating. It was a very strange sensation.

The small aliens were still moving around in consternation—Jenny could see by their feet. A bunch of them crowded between the tables and lifted Jenny back to hers.

She was positioned too high—she felt her ponytail hanging over the edge of the table. And the light above her was dimmer. Maybe somebody who hadn't been staring up at it for half an hour wouldn't notice, but Jenny did.

The blue-eyed alien with the needle was beside her.

She expected it to touch her, but it didn't. It just looked down, and Jenny looked back.

Why didn't you let me fall? she thought.

Abruptly the tall alien turned away. It motioned to the others, then walked out the octagonal doorway of the round room. Several of the small ones followed it, pushing the cart. Several others came and poured green liquid into Jenny's mouth.

It tasted like sugar and iodine. Jenny spit it out. They restrained her head and poured her mouth full again. This time she shut her lips, holding the liquid inside her mouth, doing her best not to swallow any. She could have struck out at them—she could feel her fingers again—but she pretended she couldn't move.

And then, blessedly, they went away.

Jenny turned her head and spat her mouthful out. Her lips and tongue were numb. She saw Dee doing the same.

They looked at each other, then at the lights.

"Both dimmer," Jenny whispered. Dee nodded.

Then, eyes on the doorway, they squirmed and rocked themselves off the tables. It wasn't easy, but with the lights this dim, it was possible.

Jenny, with no training in how to fall, bruised her arm and knee. But Dee was already pulling her up, out of the influence of the white light. Outside its circle, Jenny could move freely.

"Look," she said, seizing Dee's arm.

It was a door, concave, set in the wall that had been behind Jenny's head. It looked like an airplane door, which Jenny recognized because she'd once spent five hours studying one when her family flew to Florida on vacation.

And which was absurd, Jenny thought fretfully. Why should aliens have airplane doors? Dee wasn't worrying about it—she was moving levers and things. The door swung away outward.

Jenny shrieked.

She'd never liked heights, and this was much higher than she'd ever been in the open air. She could see clouds below.

But we both went for the door instinctively, she thought. It must be right. We went into Dee's room and the door disappeared. This is the first door we've seen since. It's *got* to be the way out.

She still felt faint when she looked down.

"I don't care; I'd rather die than stay here. Besides, I always wanted to skydive," Dee said, grabbed Jenny's hand, and jumped.

Jenny *really* screamed then.

Whistling wind slapped her face. Jenny's eyes screwed shut against it. Everything was icy cold around her. She felt weightless, but she knew she was falling.

If this is flying, I don't think I like it—

She didn't exactly faint then, but things got very confused. She couldn't see or hear anything until she hit an ocher-painted door with a thud, Dee tumbling behind her. From their direction and velocity they might have been thrown through Dee's bedroom window by a giant fist. The door opened as she struck it, and she and Dee both fell into the hallway.

The Haunted Mansion hallway. Dark as a crypt. Jenny stared into the golden glow of Dee's bed-room—

—then the door whisked by her nose and slammed shut.

She and Dee lay panting while their eyes gradually adjusted to the dimness. Dee leaned over and slowly, deliberately punched Jenny in the biceps.

"We did it, killer," she said. "You saved me."

"We're alive," Jenny said wonderingly. "We got through. Dee—do you realize what happened? We *won.*"

"Of course," Dee said. She poked her fingers into the hole in her leggings, and Jenny saw that the cut was still there, the blood drying. Then Dee flipped up her shirt. Jenny could count ribs under the velvety night-dark skin, below Dee's dark blue sports bra. But there was no mark above the navel. "I told you, you saved me. That was my worst nightmare—those *things* poking at me, and me not being able to stop them."

"We both did it—by using our brains," Jenny said. "Anyway, now we know what to do in the nightmares. Once we're inside we look for a door—any door. Hey, what's that?"

A scrap of paper showed white against the black carpet. Jenny smoothed it out and saw it was a drawing, done in crayons. A black thing like a bowler hat was hovering above stick trees, with rays of scribbled light around it.

"I never could draw very well," Dee said. "But you get the idea. Now what do we do?"

Fear of the aliens had left its mark on Dee's face, but she also looked exhilarated, triumphant. Ready for anything.

Jenny was suddenly very grateful to have this beautiful, brave girl on her side. "We find the others," she said. "We look for another door."

She dropped the crumpled paper on the floor and stood, offering Dee a hand up.

An unseen clock struck eleven.

Jenny stiffened. "That's it—the clock I heard in the parlor. It's counting off the hours. He said dawn was at six-eleven."

"Seven hours and change," Dee said. "Plenty of time."

Jenny said nothing, but her little fingers tingled. She couldn't explain it, but she had the feeling Dee was going to be proved very wrong.

7

The hallway seemed to stretch forever in both directions. The stairway had disappeared.

"It's changed," she said. "It keeps changing—why?"

Dee shook her head. "And who knows which way to go? We'd better separate."

Jenny nearly objected to this, but after what they'd been through—well, she should be able to handle a hallway alone. She started down it and immediately lost sight of Dee.

It seemed almost normal to be walking down an impossible black-carpeted hall like something out of a horror movie. I guess you can get used to anything, Jenny thought. After the blinding-white sterility of the alien ship, this dim place looked almost cozy.

There were no doors. Even the monster one, which should have been somewhere back this way, had disappeared. The tiny flames of the candles went on endlessly ahead. As Jenny stopped under one to rest, she thought suddenly of the riddle she'd pushed to the back of her mind earlier. If it would get one of them out of here, she ought to try to solve it.

I am just two and two. I am hot. I am cold.
I'm the parent of numbers that cannot be told.
I'm a gift beyond measure, a matter of course,
And I'm yielded with pleasure—when taken by force.

What could it possibly mean? Two and two, hot and cold—it was probably something childishly simple.

"How do you like the Game so far?" The voice was like silk-wrapped steel.

Jenny turned fast. Julian was leaning against the wall. He'd changed clothes again; he was wearing ordinary black jeans and a black T-shirt with the sleeves rolled up.

Seeing him suddenly was like the first moment in the morning when the shower flicks on, a shock of cold awareness.

"Was it you?" she said. "In the ship up there?"

"That would be telling," he said, but for an instant his eyelids drooped, heavy lashes coming down.

"Why didn't you let me fall?"

"Did you know your eyes are dark as cypress trees? That means you're unhappy. When you're happy they get lighter, they go all goldy-green."

"How would you know? You've never *seen* me happy."

He gave her a laughing glance. "Is that what you think? I'm a Shadow Man, Jenny." While Jenny was trying to figure this out, he went right on. "Cypress eyes and sun-glowing skin . . . and your hair's like liquid amber. Why do you wear it back like that?"

"Because Tom likes it," Jenny said reflexively, her standard response. "Look, what did you mean—"

He shook his head, clicking his tongue. "May I?" he said politely, straightening up. His tone was so normal, so solicitous, that Jenny nodded automatically. She was still intent on her question.

"What did you—no, *don't.*"

He had pulled the elastic band out of her ponytail. Jenny felt her hair fall about her neck, and then his fingers were in it.

An almost imperceptible shudder went through Jenny. *"Don't,"* she said again. She didn't know how to deal with this situation. He wasn't being rough. He still looked solicitous and friendly. It didn't seem appropriate to hit him in the gut as Dee had taught her to do with guys that annoyed her.

"Beautiful," he murmured. His touch was as light as the soft pat of a cat's paw, and his voice was like black velvet. "Don't you like it?"

"No," Jenny said, but she could feel the heat in her face. She was backed against the wall now. She didn't know how to get away from him—and the worst thing was that her body didn't seem sure it wanted to. His cool fingers moved against her warm hair roots, and she felt a trembling thrill.

"Have I told you about your mouth?" he said. "No? It's soft. Short upper lip, full lower. Just about perfect, except that it's usually a little wistful. There's something you want, Jenny, that you're not getting."

"I have to go now," Jenny said in a rush. Her standard stuck-with-a-jerk-at-a-party response. She was so confused she didn't care if it didn't make sense here.

"You don't have to go anywhere." He seemed unable to take his eyes away from her face for a second. Jenny had never held anyone's gaze for this long—and she had never even dreamed of eyes like his.

"I could show you what it is you've been wanting," he said. "Will you let me? Let me show you, Jenny."

His voice seemed to steal the bones from her body. She was aware of shaking her head slightly, as much in response to the new feelings as to his question. She didn't know what was happening to her. Tom's touch made her feel safe, but this—this made her feel weak inside, as if her stomach were falling.

"Let me show you," he said again, so softly she could barely hear him. His fingers were so gentle as they laced in her hair, urging her to tilt her face up toward him. His lips were bare inches from hers. Jenny felt herself flowing toward him.

"Oh, stop," she said. "Stop."

"Do you really want me to?"

"Yes."

"All right." To her astonishment, he stepped back, fingers trailing out of her hair.

Jenny could still feel them. I almost kissed him, she thought. Not the other way around. In another minute I would have.

Tom. Oh, Tom.

"Why are you *doing* this?" she said, her eyes filling again.

He sighed. "I told you. I fell in love with you. I didn't do it on purpose."

"But we're so different," Jenny whispered. She was

still feeling weak at the knees. "Why should you—want me? Why?"

He looked at her, head tilted slightly, quizzically. "Don't you know?" His eyes moved to her lips. "Light to darkness, Jenny. Darkness to light. It's always been that way."

"I don't know what you're talking about." And she didn't. She wouldn't let herself understand it.

"Suppose the devil was just quietly minding his own business—when he saw a girl. A girl who made him forget everything. There've been other girls more beautiful, of course—but this girl had *something*. A goodness, a sweetness about her. An innocence. Something simple he wanted."

"To destroy it."

"No, no. To cherish it. To warm his cold heart. Even a poor devil can dream, can't he?"

"You're trying to trick me."

"Am I?" There was something oddly serious in his blue eyes.

"I won't listen to you. You can't make me listen."

"True." For just an instant Julian looked tired. Then he gave his strange half smile. "Then there's no choice but to keep playing, is there? No choice for either of us."

"Julian—"

"What?"

Jenny caught herself up short, shaking her head.

He was crazy. But one thing she believed, he really was in love with her. She knew, somehow, that it was true. She also knew something else about him— she'd known it since that instant when she'd looked into his eyes and seen the ancient shadows there.

She'd known it when he'd humiliated Tom and terrorized Dee.

He was evil. Cruel, capricious, and dangerous as a cobra. A prince of darkness.

Completely evil—and completely in love with her.

How was she supposed to reconcile that?

"If you want me so much," she said, "why don't you just *take* me, then? Why go through all this with the Game? You could grab me anytime—why don't you just do it?"

His heavy lashes drooped again. In that instant he looked exactly like the boy in the More Games store. Almost vulnerable—almost human.

Realization came to Jenny. "Because you can't," she breathed. "You can't, can you? You can't do just *anything* you want to, not even here."

His eyes flashed up, glittering like a snake's. Jenny saw pure violence there. "This is *my* world. I make the rules here—"

"No." Giddy triumph was swelling through Jenny, an effervescent rush. "Not this one. That's why you asked if you could touch my hair. That's why you tried to make *me* kiss *you*. You can't do it without my permission."

"Be careful, Jenny," he said. His face was cold and cruel.

Jenny just laughed excitedly. "If you can kiss me against my will, then prove it," she said. "Show me—do it now." And then she added an Italian phrase she'd picked up from Audrey. *"Come osi!"*

It meant *I dare you.*

He didn't move.

Jenny laughed again.

"I don't think you understand," he said. "I'm going to have you, at any cost. *Any* cost, Jenny, even if you have to suffer on the way. If I can't force you, I'll persuade you—and I can be very persuasive."

Jenny felt some of the triumph fold up inside her.

"Remember where you are, Jenny. Whose territory you're on. Remember what I can do in the Game."

Jenny was completely sober now.

"You challenged me—now I suppose I'll have to show you what I *am* capable of."

"I don't care what you do to me."

"Maybe it won't be to you. See your friend there? She's playing the Game, too."

He was looking down the hallway, in the same direction Jenny had been going. Barely visible under a far candle was the copper glint of someone's hair. Jenny drew in her breath.

"Don't you dare—" Turning back to speak to him, Jenny broke off. Julian was gone. She was alone.

Jenny bit her lip. It was infuriating to talk to somebody who could do that, and she was beginning to think it hadn't been a very good idea to laugh at him. Nothing to be done about it now.

"Audrey!" she called and started down the hall.

Audrey's skin, usually pale as magnolia blossoms, was touched with a golden glow from the candles, and her auburn hair flashed copper. She and Jenny hugged, and Jenny thought only Audrey could stay so calm, so chic, in such awful circumstances.

"You look as if any minute you're going to be demanding to see your ambassador," Jenny said.

"If Daddy were here he'd take care of things," Audrey agreed. "He'd come out of retirement to take this place on. Are you all right? You look a little flushed."

Jenny put a hand to her cheek self-consciously. "It's the light," she said. "Uh, how long have you been here? I mean, did you see me—before I called?"

"No. I'd been looking and looking—for *anybody,* but all I've seen is this *interminable* hallway."

"Good. I mean—it's good that I found you. The only other person I've seen is Dee. She's back there, and she's just been through hell. And you're next, if I'm right about the way this works. I'll explain as we go."

The explanation, about how they were all scattered, about finding doors in the nightmares, about the dawn time limit and about how things in the nightmares could hurt you, took until they found Dee. They did find Dee, to Jenny's relief, standing beside a door.

"I thought I'd better guard it to make sure it didn't go anywhere," she said after a perfunctory nod at Audrey.

Audrey had only one question. "Is he Nordic, that guy? They're supposed to be sexy as all get-out."

Jenny ignored this. "Since the doors move, how do we know this isn't one of the two we opened before?"

"We don't," Dee said and flashed The Smile. Dee's wild, leaping beauty always annoyed Audrey. "Of course, it doesn't have a key like the first one, but I guess we'd better get in monster position again. Anything could be inside."

She and Jenny did, ready to kick the door shut fast. Audrey's eyebrows lifted into her spiky bangs. "No, thank you," she said politely. "Not in a fitted linen skirt. Listen, you two, why are we doing this at all? Why don't we just sit down and refuse to play?"

"Didn't you listen to me before?" Jenny said. "If we're still here by dawn, we stay for good. We lose automatically."

"I've never lost *anything* by default," Dee said. Then she said, *"Now."*

Behind the door there was a forest.

Cool wind blew out, ruffling Jenny's loose hair against her cheek. It smelled like summer camp.

"God," said Jenny.

"Well, come on," Audrey said, flicking her perfectly polished nails in a gesture of readiness. "We might as well get it over with."

"It's too weird," Jenny said as they stepped inside —outside. "Dee's bedroom was a *room*, at least. But this . . ."

They were on the outskirts of a dark forest on a sloping hill. Above them the night sky was strewn with stars much bigger and brighter than the ones Jenny usually saw from her Vista Grande backyard. A moon of pure silver was rising.

The door had slammed and disappeared, of course, as soon as they stepped through. Behind Jenny were meadows and pastures; before her a tangled mass of pitch-black trunks and bushes. The girls were alone on the hill in the moonlight.

"Now what?" Audrey said, shivering fastidiously.

"Don't you know? It's your nightmare—you drew it."

"I drew a picture of me opening the Bloomies catalog and finding it *blank*," Audrey said. "That's

my worst nightmare. Don't look at me that way—
shopping is cheaper than therapy."

And that was all she would say about it.

There were a few scattered lights in the valley
below them. "But it's too far to hike," Jenny said,
"and even if we did get down there, I don't think that
there would really be any people."

Audrey looked at her strangely, but Dee nodded.

"It feels like one of those model-train landscapes
—or like a stage set," she said. "False fronts. You're
right, I don't think we'd find little houses with people
in them down there. Which means—"

They faced the forest bleakly.

"Why do I have a bad feeling about this?" Jenny
asked.

"Come on," Dee said. "Let's make it happen."

The forest looked solid, but with Dee in the lead
they found a way into it. It was mostly pine and fir
trees, with the occasional beech shining silvery gray
against the darkness of the background.

"Oh, my God," Audrey said after they'd been
walking some time. "High ground, evergreen trees,
rocks—I know where we are now. It's the Black
Forest."

"Sounds like something from a story," Jenny
muttered, picking her way through the undergrowth.

"It's a real place. I saw it when I was eight, when
Daddy was at the German embassy. It—scared me a
little, because it was *the* forest, you know."

Dee threw a derisive glance over her shoulder.
"The forest?"

"The forest where everything happened—where
the Grimm brothers got all their fairy tales. You

know, Snow White. Hänsel and Gretel. Little Red Riding-Hood and the—"

Audrey stopped in midsentence. In front of her, Dee had stopped, too. Jenny's knees locked.

Just ahead of them in the tangled blackness, yellow eyes glowed. Jenny even imagined she could see moonlight gleaming off sharp teeth.

All three girls stood very still. Seconds passed and the yellow eyes remained motionless. Then they seemed to shift to a different angle so that one went out. Both flashed toward the girls again, then both went out. Jenny heard underbrush crunching. The sound got fainter. It faded into a profound silence in which Jenny could hear her heart beating strong and very fast in her chest.

Jenny let out her breath.

Dee's shoulders heaved slightly. She reached down and picked up a long stick almost as thick as her own slim wrist. She settled it in her hand, waggling it, testing her grip. It made a good weapon.

"—and the Wolf," said Audrey, her voice suspiciously calm. She tucked stray wisps of hair into her French twist, her lips tight. The three of them looked at one another, then started walking again. What else was there to do?

"It was strange, that wolf coming just when you were talking about one," Dee said.

"Unless—" Jenny stopped dead. "Wait," she said. Something had fallen into place with an almost audible click. "Let me think a minute . . . *yes*. It wasn't strange at all that the wolf came when Audrey was talking about it. Don't you see? He's taking it all from our own minds."

"Who?" Audrey said, her well-bred nostrils flared.

"Who do you think? Julian. The Shadow Man. He's creating the Game around us—or *we're* doing it—but either way it's made up of our own thoughts. That hallway back in the house is the hallway from the Haunted Mansion at Disneyland. It always scared me as a kid—so it came from *my* mind. And the door in the UFO was like a plane door I'd seen."

Dee's eyes flashed like a jaguar's. "And the parlor—I saw a lamp like that once in Jamestown. I wondered what it was doing here."

"Everything—every detail—is coming from us," Jenny said. "Not just big things but little things. He's using our minds against us."

"So what's going to happen next?" Dee asked Audrey. "You're the one who should know what scares you most. I mean, should we be on the lookout for walking trees or little hooded men or what? Or was that wolf it?"

"I was only eight when I lived here," Audrey said coldly. "And, no, I don't remember specifically which story . . . disturbed me . . . most. I had a German nurse, and she told me all of them."

She and Dee glared at each other.

"We could run into something from any of our minds," Jenny said, to make peace. "Anything could happen here. You can feel it."

She knew in her heart that it was going to be something worse than the wolf. Something more *un-mundane*. Audrey didn't like anything supernatural, so it followed that whatever happened was going to be *very*.

Remember, it's all a dream, she told herself. But she could hear Julian's voice in her mind: *"I can tell you right off that one of you probably won't make it."*

They walked. Underbrush clutched at Jenny's skirt like little fingers. The fragrance of evergreens surrounded them like a thousand Christmas trees. All Jenny could see was darkness and the endless tangle of forest ahead. Her nerves stretched and stretched.

They literally stumbled on the clearing.

One large tree grew there—a yew, Jenny thought. It stood in front of a great jumble of rocks and boulders that looked as if they might have been left by a glacier. The tree had rough bark, dark green needles, and red berries.

Gathered around it was a group of young men in weird clothes.

They were wearing pants and long over-tunics of leather trimmed with fur, very old-fashioned looking. Their arms were bare and muscular. The ground beside the tree had been cleared and a circle drawn on it. Inside the circle a fire burned, and red light glinted off daggers and what looked like drinking horns. The whole area was decorated with flowers.

"It's some kind of secret ceremony," Dee whispered. "And we're spying on it," she added with considerable relish.

"They're certainly good-looking," Audrey murmured.

They were. Jenny counted seven of them, four with blond hair and three with blondish-brown. They looked as if they were in their late teens or early twenties, and if what they were doing was secret, they weren't bothering to be quiet about it. Jenny could hear laughter and boisterous singing.

Good grief, it's like a fraternity party, she thought. Even this far away she could smell the beer.

"I think," said Audrey, "I'm beginning to like this Game."

She stepped out before Jenny could stop her. The singing fell silent. Seven faces turned toward the girls. Then one of the German boys lifted a drinking horn over his head, and all the rest cheered.

They all seemed surprised but delighted to see the girls. White, even teeth flashed in friendly smiles, and they bundled the visitors over to the warmth of the fire. Audrey's bare legs caused a lot of appreciative comment, as did Dee's spandex leggings.

"No—no, thanks," Jenny said as one of them tried to get her to drink the stuff in his horn. The horn had angular symbols carved on it that made her nervous somehow—they reminded her of something. "Audrey, what are they *saying?*"

"I can't catch it all. It's not like the German I learned," Audrey said. Seated between two admirers, her cool porcelain beauty contrasted with her flirtatious lashes. "I think it must be archaic. But that one is saying that you're like Sif. It's a compliment—Sif was a goddess with shining golden hair."

"Oh, give me a break!" Dee backed up to sit on a rock.

There was an instant stirring among the German boys. Several pulled Dee away from the rock pile, shaking their heads. Dee barely allowed them to move her, not at all placated by the way they marveled over her dark skin. And she only snorted when one offered her a garland of flowers to wear.

"Oh, put it on," Jenny said, flicking a small bug out of her own wreath. She was starting to enjoy this. The young men were nice, even if they did smell a bit

97

like sweat. They were about the most strapping youths she'd ever seen, but several of them had braids in their hair, and they didn't seem to think weaving garlands was sissy.

"It's a ceremony to greet the spring," Audrey said as one of the blonds cried, *"Ostara!"* and poured beer on the ground. "Ostara's the goddess of spring—that's where we get 'Easter.'"

The young men began to chant.

"It's something about life being renewed," Audrey said. "There's something else—something I can't quite make out. They're . . . asking? Petitioning?"

All the German boys were on their feet by now, urging the girls to rise. They were facing the huge pile of boulders.

"Dokkalfar," they chanted.

"That's dark—something. I don't—*oh, my God."* Audrey's voice changed completely. She tried to pull away from the circle, but two of the German boys grabbed her. "Dark *elves,"* she said wildly. "That's what they're saying. They came here to ask favors from the elves—and *we're* the yielding."

Jenny had never heard Audrey's voice like that before—bordering on hysteria. "The what?" she demanded. Suddenly the white, even smiles around her didn't look so friendly.

"The gift to the Otherworld. The *sacrifice!"* Audrey cried. She was trying to get away again, but it was no good.

We're outnumbered more than two to one, Jenny thought. And they've all got muscles. She looked at Dee—and felt shock ripple over her. Dee was laughing.

Snickering, actually. Chortling. "Elves?" she

gasped. "Little pixies in bluebells? Little guys who sit on acorns?"

"No, you idiot," Audrey said through her teeth. "Dark elves—Outdwellers. Oh, you don't understand—"

Jenny heard rock scraping. One of the huge stones in front of her was *moving*. It swung out slowly, pushing a ridge of dirt along in front of it. A black, gaping hole was revealed in the pile. A tunnel leading down.

Dee's laughter was dying—but it was too late. The girls were pushed forward into the hole. Jenny tried to turn, but her Capezio flats slithered on dust and grit, and she felt herself falling.

8

Rock scraped on rock and the moonlight was cut off above them. Audrey was lying in a ball beside Jenny near the bottom of the slope. Dee had been shoved in backward and was sprawled at the very bottom, legs higher than her head. In those first moments Jenny didn't stop to wonder how she could still see either of them. She said, "Are you all right?" to Dee and then wrapped her arms around Audrey comfortingly.

Audrey was *shaking*. Making little moaning sounds.

"I'm sorry, I'm so sorry. . . ." Jenny said, hugging her.

"It's not *your* fault." Dee was picking herself up, her fine-boned face contemptuous. "What's her problem, anyway?"

Jenny twisted her head to snap at Dee, but the words never got out. She could now see the reason they weren't in pitch darkness. There was a semicircle of lanterns around the bottom of the slope, and holding the lanterns were people.

Dee had fallen silent. The lantern light reflected off faces that were disturbing to say the least.

The elves were very pale, very beautiful . . . but very strange. Their eyes were slanted in a way that reminded Jenny of the Visitors'. Their cheekbones were almost too high and sharp. And they stood oddly.

They didn't look as if they had any sympathy to appeal to.

One of them said something. Jenny thought it was the same language that the young men outside had used, but the elf's voice was more liquid—and more cold. It was obvious that he was ordering the girls up.

Jenny didn't want to obey. She was irrationally frightened by these pale beautiful people. Then she saw that maybe her fear wasn't so irrational.

They were like animals—or parts of them were. They were deformed.

The elf who had spoken had one normal hand and one hand like a cow's split hoof. It was black and shiny like patent leather. Jenny was afraid she was going to be sick.

Another of them had a tail hanging out of his breeches—a long, pink naked tail like a rat's. It swished. A third had two little horn-buds swelling on his forehead. A fourth had glossy dark hair growing on his neck.

Every one of them had some deformity. And they were *real*. Not like the pasted-together monstrosities Jenny had seen in the Ripley's Believe It or Not! exhibit.

"Audrey, you've got to get up," she whispered, swallowing the bile that had risen in her throat. "Audrey, if you don't I think they'll *make* you." Then, with desperate inspiration: "Do you want them to see you lying here like this? I bet your mascara's smeared halfway down your face."

The appeal to Audrey's pride worked where nothing else might have. She slowly sat up, brushing at her cheeks.

"It's waterproof," she said defiantly. Her fingers went automatically to adjust the combs in her French twist, and then she saw the elves.

Her chestnut eyes widened until they showed white all around. She was staring at the cow's-hoof hand. Jenny gripped her arm tightly.

"Are they what you thought they were?"

Audrey pressed her lips together and nodded.

The elf spoke again, sharply, stepping forward. Audrey cringed back. Slowly and carefully Jenny urged her to stand.

"Audrey, we've got to go with them," she whispered. She was afraid that if Audrey balked, the elves were going to *touch* them. The thought of that—of being touched by that shiny hoof or by the flipper she saw one of the others had—was more than Jenny could bear. "Please, Audrey," she whispered.

It was easy for the elves to lead them. All they had to do was close in from one direction, and the girls would move in the other.

They walked like that, surrounded by a circle of lanterns, down a passage that sloped on and on. Other passages branched away. Clearly the place was big—and they were going deeper and deeper into it.

Walking calmed Jenny a little. The rocks around

them took every imaginable shape—some like twisting antlers, others like windblown grass. There were lacy falls of angel hair, and huge columns covered with formations like exquisite flowers or the gills of mushrooms.

The air smelled like rain-damp earth. It was surprisingly warm.

Jenny tightened her supporting grip on Audrey's arm.

"Say something to them," she suggested. "Ask them where we're going."

In her own way Audrey was as brave as Dee. Her spiky eyelashes were starred together from crying, and she didn't look at the elf beside her. But she spoke to him in level tones.

"He says they're taking us to the Erlking," she said after a moment. Now Jenny could hear taut, shaking control in her voice. "That means—elf king, I think. I remember the story about the Erlking now. He's a kind of evil spirit who haunts the Black Forest. He's supposed to—take people. Especially young girls and children."

Dee pounced. "Why girls?"

Audrey spoke between clenched teeth. "You guess. But all the dark elves are that way. Well, *look* at them. They're all men. It's a male race."

With a shock, Jenny realized that it was true. The delicacy of their features had fooled her. Every one of their captors was beautiful—and male.

Dee's grin was bloodthirsty. "Time to fight."

"No," Jenny said tensely. Her heart was pounding, but she tried to quiet it. "There are too many of them; we wouldn't have a chance. And anyway, we're supposed to *face* our nightmares, remember? If the

Erlking is what Audrey's most afraid of, he must be what we have to face."

"It's a *stupid* nightmare anyway," Dee hissed, her supple shoulders hunching as if an ice cube were going down her back.

"Believe me," Audrey said bitingly, "I wish you weren't in it with me."

The two girls ignored each other as they walked on through subterranean caverns of cathedral spaciousness. Glittering white gypsum crystals powdered everything, catching the lantern light. Coarse rock dust crunched underneath Jenny's feet.

"I don't understand," Audrey whispered. "This can't have come out of my mind. I've never seen anything like it."

"I have," Dee said, and even her voice was subdued. "Spelunking in New Mexico. But it wasn't so—*much.*"

At last they reached the biggest cavern of all.

They passed giant red pillars like coral reefs which gave Jenny the disconcerting feeling of being underwater.

They were heading straight for an enormous wall of flame-colored rock. It wasn't flat. It went rippling up and up like an inverted Niagara Falls. At floor level there was an irregularly shaped gap in the wall—like an entrance.

"The castle," Audrey translated quietly.

They passed through the gap in the red walls.

Inside, the elves moved to separate the girls into two groups. It happened so fast that Jenny didn't have time to react. All in an instant she was being herded away, and when she twisted her head frantically she saw Dee and Audrey being borne in the opposite direction. She saw Audrey's copper head bobbing and heard Dee's voice raised in fury. Then Dee's voice faded, and Jenny was led through a gap into a large room.

One of her captors said something ending with *"Erlkönig,"* and they all walked out. When Jenny looked through the gap, she found they were standing sentry on either side.

Now what?

She looked around. The rock formations here were like huge sand castles, half melted by water, in white and gold. Jenny realized she was seeing by moonlight and looked up. The ceiling had openings in it like skylights or chimneys in the rock. She studied them for a while.

Finally there was nothing to do but wait—and worry. What was happening to Tom right now? she wondered.

Think about the riddle, she told herself firmly. It'll pass the time, and it might be useful.

I am just two and two. I am hot. I am cold.
I'm the parent of numbers that cannot be told.
I'm a gift beyond measure, a matter of course,
And I'm yielded with pleasure—when taken by
    force.

Suddenly she had it. Yes! Something that could be hot and passionate or cold and impersonal. Something that could be the "parent" of untold numbers of people—because there was no counting how many babies had gotten started with it. Something

105

that was just two and two—two lips touching two lips.

A kiss.

Jenny smiled in triumph. She'd solved the riddle. She could get one of the others free.

There was no question, of course, about who it would be. Much as she loved her friends, Tom would always come first.

The only problem with having solved the riddle was that she now had nothing to think about—except whatever was going to happen to her. The elf who'd left had said *"Erlkönig."* The Erlking? Was that who she was waiting for?

What kind of deformity would the Erlking have? she wondered. Hooves? Horns?

If he's king, he probably has something worse than all the others, she thought, and her heart chilled.

Someone came through the gap in the stone, and Jenny braced herself. The next minute she realized how dense she'd been.

He was wearing a white tunic and breeches and soft white boots. They showed off how lithe and smoothly muscled he was. In the moonlight his hair was silver as a mirror, and he was smiling.

"Julian."

"Welcome," he said, "to the Erlking's castle."

The last time they had spoken, Jenny had been furious with him. It was hard to keep that in mind now. The white leather was so soft looking, and it clung to him, hip and thigh. And there was something about a guy who looked at you with eyes like a starving tiger's. All at once Jenny felt disconcerted.

Tom always looked so good in ordinary clothes—

but he was very conservative, never would dress up even at Halloween. Julian, by contrast, obviously got off on outrageous.

His broad leather belt showed how flat his stomach was, emphasized his narrow hips. It was modestly encrusted with sapphires. Jenny wished she had one like it.

"The Erlking, huh? Enjoying the part?"

"Immensely," Julian assured her gravely.

"At least you're *talking* to me in this nightmare. Not like the UFO one, I mean."

"Jenny. I will happily talk to you all night."

"Thank you, but there's a time limit, and I'd rather have my friends back."

"Say the word."

Jenny looked at him, startled, and then realized what word he meant. "No," she said. "I'll do it the hard way. We're going to get through all the nightmares, you know. We're going to win the Game."

"I admire your confidence."

"You can admire my success—starting now. I've solved your riddle, and you're a male chauvinist pig. It is *not* given with pleasure when taken by force."

"What isn't?"

"A kiss." She turned to face him fully. "That's the answer, isn't it? And you told me if I solved the riddle, you'd let one of my friends go."

"Wrong." He waited for her reaction, eyes glinting in a wicked smile. "I told you if you *gave me* the answer, I'd let one of your friends go. But you haven't *given* it to me yet." His eyes lingered on her lips. "Would you like to now?"

Fury sparked in Jenny. "You—!" She turned away

so he wouldn't have the satisfaction of seeing her angry.

"I've upset you. You're offended," he said. He sounded genuinely penitent. Jenny couldn't keep up with these mercurial changes of mood. "Here, I'll give you something to make it up to you."

Reluctantly Jenny turned again. He was holding a rose—a white rose. Or maybe it was silver—in this light it was hard to tell. It was the most beautiful thing she'd ever seen.

As she took it, Jenny realized it wasn't real but was exquisitely wrought, perfect down to the tiniest detail. Half opened, the blossom shimmered in her hands. The petals were cool but soft.

"Made from silver dug out by black elves in the deepest mines of the earth," Julian said. Jenny shook her head at him.

"That's all *folklore*. Are you saying you're *really* the Erlking? Do you want me to believe in Hänsel and Gretel, too?"

"I've been more things than you can imagine. And what I want you to believe is that children can go into dark places and disappear. After which people might tell stories to explain it—sometimes true stories, sometimes not."

Jenny felt disconcerted again. "Anyway—it's a beautiful rose," she said and stroked it against her cheek.

Julian's eyes gleamed.

"Let's go walking in the courtyard," he said. "You can really see the moonlight there."

The courtyard had a number of natural chimneys, and moonlight flooded down. Jenny felt almost awestruck at the beauty of the landscape. The moonlight threw a sort of magic sheen over everything, and the cavern was weirdly beautiful with its dark shadows and bright patches of silver.

Julian looked the same. Every shadow on his face was dead black, and there were silver points in his eyes.

"Have you ever wondered why you can go into dangerous places without getting hurt?" he said abruptly. "Why the stray animals you pick up never bite you, why you don't get mugged—or worse—when you wander around bad parts of town at night?"

"I . . ." People were always yelling at Jenny for exactly the things he was talking about. She herself had never given it much thought, but now a wild suspicion was rising in her mind. "No," she said. "No, I haven't."

His eyes remained on hers. "I've been looking after you, Jenny. Watching over you. No one can touch you . . . no one but me."

"That's impossible." It came out in a whisper. "You . . . I've done those things all my life. . . ." Her sentences were coming untangled.

"And I couldn't have been watching you that long? But I have. I've always loved you, Jenny."

The power of his gaze was frightening. Jenny was confused by her own emotions. She knew she should feel only hatred, only anger toward him, but by now she had to admit that part of her was fascinated by him. He was a prince of darkness—

—who had chosen *her.*

She turned and walked away from him, trying to gather herself.

"I have never been in love before," Julian said. "You're my first—and you'll be my only."

There was music in his voice, and the words settled like filigreed snowflakes around her, wrapping her in otherworldliness.

Jenny turned around and he touched her.

His touch was as tenuous as gauze on her cheek. Jenny was so surprised she didn't move. Then she looked down stupidly. He had taken her hand.

But I thought you couldn't . . .

His fingertips were as cool as jade against her skin. Tingles followed in their wake. She had an urge to press her cheek to his open hand.

Don't, she thought. Don't, don't, don't . . .

"Don't," she whispered.

He went on stroking her hand, thumb gently circling in her palm. A sensuous and dangerous feeling. Jenny felt herself start to come undone.

His touch was so delicate—he'd disengaged her hand so gently from the rose. . . .

From the rose, Jenny thought.

His gift. She'd held it in her hand. She'd stroked it against her right cheek—the cheek he was touching now.

She stepped back. "You . . . tricked me."

He still held her hand. "Does it matter?"

"Yes, it *matters,*" Jenny said furiously, trying to pull out of his grasp. How could she have been so stupid? It was a game he was playing with her, to get permission to touch more and more of her. "I understand now—I'll never touch you or anything you give me. That trick won't work again."

His lips were smiling, but there was something hot and deadly serious in his eyes. "Maybe not—but another one will. Believe me, Jenny: I'm going to make you mine—entirely—before you finish the Game."

Jenny wished she could think of something more mature to say than, "In your dreams!"

"No—in yours," he said. "And remember, you're not alone here."

Jenny heard a scream.

"That's Audrey," she said. "That's Audrey! Something's happening to her!" When he wouldn't release her hand, she jerked it out of his.

Then she saw his eyes—and what she saw there froze her.

"You know," she whispered. "You're *doing* it—to get back at me."

"I warned you," he said. The screaming was still going on. "Do you want it to stop?"

Evil, she thought. Absolute evil. Cruel, capricious, and dangerous as a cobra. I won't forget that again.

"I'll stop it myself," she said, her voice soft but fierce. "I told you I was going to win this Game. And I am. And I will *never* give in to you."

She threw the silver rose at his feet.

Then she was running for the sound of Audrey's screams.

Elves rushed at her as she plunged out of the sandcastle room, but she veered sharply and got by them. Audrey's screams were getting clearer and clearer. Jenny saw a gap in the nearest red wall and ducked into it, and suddenly the screams echoed all around her.

She saw Audrey sitting and Dee standing in front of her. She stumbled the last few feet to collapse beside them.

"What's wrong?"

Audrey was half sitting, half lying against the gypsum-encrusted wall of a small cavern. Her features were contorted with horror—and when Jenny turned she saw why.

She would have thought that after all she'd been through, she would be inured to weird creatures. But these things—these things were—

"Oh, *God*, Audrey, what are they?" she choked out.

Audrey's fingernails bit into Jenny's arm. "They're *draugar*. Living corpses. They've come for us. I—" She turned away, retching.

They *smelled* like corpses—the sickly-sweet odor of decay. Some of them had bloated bodies. Some had leathery skin, fallen in and wrinkled. Some, to Jenny's horror, had skin that was sloughing off.

One had thick fingernails turned brown by time and grown into long, dangling spirals. The nails clattered together, making a sound that raised gooseflesh all over Jenny's body.

They were completely blocking the exit. Jenny didn't know how she'd gotten around them to reach Audrey, but there was no getting out again. They were closing in from all sides.

"When I tell you, run for the door!" Dee said.

"What door?"

Dee pointed and Jenny turned. Beyond the nearest *draugr* on the right was a wall—and there was a door in it. A Gothic door with an arched top, painted blue.

"Okay?" Dee shouted. "Get ready for it!"

She had been standing with her left leg back, knee bent, all her weight on it. Her right leg was so bent that only the toe touched the floor. It made her look like a ballerina, but it was called the cat stance—Dee was always trying to teach Jenny kung fu stances.

Suddenly she kicked, her right foot snapping up flat to strike the *draugr* under the jaw with her heel.

With a dry crack the *draugr*'s head fell backward —all the way backward. Its neck was snapped.

The terrible thing was that it kept walking. Head resting on its own shoulder blades, blundering the wrong way, *it kept walking*.

Jenny let go and screamed.

"Get up!" Dee shouted to them. "Now, while I've got them distracted. Get out of here!"

Audrey remained frozen. "We can't leave you—"

"Don't worry about me! Just go! Jenny, take her!"

Jenny obeyed the tone of command instinctively. She hauled Audrey up by her houndstooth jacket and pulled her to the door. She wrenched it open, and they both fell through.

It slammed behind them before Jenny could stop it. She and Audrey looked at each other in dismay.

And then they waited.

They waited until a sick feeling in Jenny's stomach told her Dee wasn't going to come. Audrey was crying. Jenny tried the door handle. It wouldn't budge.

"It's my fault," Audrey whispered.

"One of you probably won't make it. . . ."

The door flew open. Dee charged through, slammed it behind her, leaned on it. She expelled a great gust of air.

"That was *close,*" she said. "But I've been dying for a fight, and it was a good one."

She was glowing with exertion and the joy of battle. She looked at Audrey.

"Well, aren't you a mess," she said.

Audrey's glossy auburn hair was hanging around her face; her spiky bangs were plastered damply to her forehead. Her cheeks were flushed and wet, her hands and legs scratched and scraped. Her cherry lipstick was gone.

Face inscrutable, Audrey held out one hand and slowly unclenched the fingers. On her palm were the combs from her French twist. "At least I still have these," she said calmly.

All three of them burst into hysterical laughter. They laughed and laughed in a violent release of emotion.

"I guess that counts as winning: getting out of your nightmare alive with your combs intact," Dee gasped finally.

Audrey raised her eyebrows, and then her lips curled again in a smile. She and Dee were smiling at each other.

An unseen clock struck twelve.

"Midnight," Jenny said. It came out softly, almost a whisper. Every time they won, that clock chimed to remind them that time was passing—passing fast. Where *was* it, anyway? The sound seemed to pervade the entire house.

"Six hours until dawn," Dee was saying to Audrey. "And only five nightmares to go. We're fine. We'll make it, easy."

"Easy? I don't *think* so," Audrey said.

"Look," Jenny said quietly, bending to pick up a scrap of paper.

9

It was an abstract rendition of a forest, very heavy on green swirling lines.

"All right, so I did draw a forest," Audrey said. "I've always had nightmares about them, but I never knew why. I didn't even know *what* forest I was scared of."

"He picks up on our subconscious," said Dee.

"So what happened to you two after we got separated?" Jenny asked.

"Not much," Dee said. "They put us in that room, only there wasn't any door at first. Then we saw the door—and at that exact instant those corpses appeared and Audrey started screaming. What about you? Did you see the Erlking?"

Jenny looked away. "Sort of. It was Julian, playing the part." She hesitated, then blurted, "You *do* know that it's because of me you're suffering, don't you? It's me he wants. He told me that he'd stop hurting you if I—if I let him—"

"Don't you *dare,*" Dee said, sloe eyes flashing.

"Don't even think about it," said Audrey with equal heat.

Jenny nodded, feeling warmth in her eyes. To cover it up she watched Audrey. While they were talking, Audrey had efficiently put her hair back up, fished a quilted pouch out of her jacket pocket, and deftly restored her cherry lipstick. Audrey had always seemed so cosmopolitan, so invulnerable—but now Jenny had seen beneath the facade.

"It must have been hard, living in all those different countries," she said slowly and glanced over at Dee.

Audrey paused a moment in the midst of fluffing her bangs. She snapped her compact shut with a click.

"Frankly, it was awful," she said. "You can't imagine the culture shock. The dislocation—the insecurity—and you never know when you're going to move again. Even now that Daddy's retired I still feel—"

"Like it's hard to make real friends?"

Audrey nodded. "I feel as if we might be picking up and going again any minute."

"You're not, though," Jenny said. "You're staying here with us." She glanced at Dee again. "Right?"

"Oh, naturally," Dee said, but there was no rancor in her voice, and she laid a slender dark hand on Audrey's back.

"You know, I don't understand," Jenny said suddenly. "Those guys in the forest seemed nice—so why did they do it? Why did they hand us over?"

"Well—elves are supposed to do people favors. Answer questions, do work for you. But they always

117

want something in return, and if you call them up and try to trap them, they sometimes trap *you*. Take you to their world. I guess those guys figured we were more expendable than they were."

Jenny nodded. "One more thing—"

"Always one more thing!" said Dee.

"—which of you did the door? I know *I* didn't put it there because I've never seen a door like that."

"I did, I suppose," said Audrey. "I saw doors like that in Germany—but I didn't *put* it there. It just appeared."

"You can't change things here by using your mind," Dee said. "You have to deal with everything here as if it's real."

"But where *is* here?" Audrey said bleakly.

"Good question," said Jenny. "It's nowhere on Earth; I know that from what I saw out the window."

"The Shadow World," Dee said. "Remember the instructions? A world that's like ours but different, that exists alongside ours, but never touches it."

" 'Some people call it the world of dreams, but it is as real as anything else. . . .' " Jenny quoted. "Well, it touched our world tonight, anyway. What's wrong now, Audrey?"

"It just occurred to me. You know, in Norse and German legends there are supposed to be nine worlds—our world's just the one in the middle."

"Nine?" said Jenny.

"Nine. There's Asgard, which is a sort of heaven, and Hel, which is a sort of hell, and a world of primal fire and a world of primal water and a world of primal wind—but, listen. There's also a world of primal ice. It's sort of connected to Hel—*and it's also a world of shadows.* It's called Niflheim, and *nifl* means 'dark, shadowy.'"

"Just what are you getting at?" Dee asked.

"I don't know. It's just strange, *nicht wahr?* God, I'm starting to think in German. But it *is* strange, isn't it—with him calling himself the Shadow Man? And I just remembered something else. The things that live in Niflheim are supposed to be terribly destructive, so they're under a rune of restraint to keep them from getting out of their world and into other peoples'. I don't remember which rune, though."

"You're *not* saying runes are real," Jenny said. "I mean, like the one Julian talked about—the one that 'pierced the veil between the worlds.' They can't really work."

"I always assumed they didn't, that it was just a silly superstition. But now . . . I don't know. They work in *legends* all right, to let you—oh, what do they call it? Fare forth between the worlds. Or summon up things from the other ones. The way those German boys summoned the elves."

The talk was making Jenny very uncomfortable. She didn't know why, and that made her even more uncomfortable. Something to do with runes, a long time ago. After all she had seen, why should it upset her that runes might be real? That day in her grandfather's basement . . .

"Look," she said abruptly, "we've been standing here gabbing forever. Don't you think we'd better start looking for the next person? There *is* a time limit, you know."

"Right," Dee said, always ready for action. "Do you want to split up again?"

"No," Jenny said quickly. "Let's stick together."
By whatever weird laws operated in this place, she'd
already yielded Julian the right to touch her hand,
her cheek, her hair. And he'd made it plain that he
wouldn't be satisfied until he got all of her, bit by bit.
It was just a question of what kind of ruse or threat
he planned to try next. Jenny figured her best chance
was not to be caught alone.

They found Michael on the third sweep down the
hall. He was wandering back and forth in front of a
door, running his hands through his rumpled dark
hair and muttering. He brightened considerably at
the sight of the girls.

"Audrey, at last! It seems like years!"

"Oh, I've been counting the seconds we've been
apart," Audrey said, raising an eyebrow and dim-
pling at the same time.

"Me, too. I only wish I had a calculator to keep
track."

And neither of them meant a word of it. Lucky for
them, thought Jenny. Love for Tom was like an
aching bruise in her chest. If only she could see him,
just for a moment . . .

They explained to Michael everything that had
happened to them. He told them that for him the
parlor had simply disappeared while Tom was cowering from the invisible creatures. Then he'd found
himself in front of this door. He'd tried the knob, but
it wouldn't open. He'd been pacing the hallway ever
since.

"And you never saw a staircase?" Jenny asked.

"No staircase, no other doors, no nothing. No
people, until you came."

"And yet we've been walking this hallway for

hours, and we've seen three doors, and I came up a staircase," Jenny said. "It's just one more weird thing about this place."

"Which we don't have time to discuss," Dee said. "Let's move, people. Who wants to try this door?"

"This time let's try to keep it open after we go in," Jenny said. "That is, if we don't need to slam it shut fast."

"We can't go in at all—it's locked," Michael said.

Dee flashed him a grin as she took up a heel stance, ready to do a forward kick. "Bets?"

The door opened easily when Jenny twisted the knob, and no monsters jumped out. Dee caught it as it swung and held it against the wall. Through the opening Jenny could see dimness.

"Uh, you first. I'm a registered coward," Michael said.

Jenny took a deep breath, squared her shoulders, and stepped over the threshold—

—into a hallway identical to the one she had left. She looked up and down it in bewilderment.

"What's going on? This door wants to close," Dee called.

"It's—" Jenny gave up and beckoned Audrey and Michael in.

"It's the same place," Audrey said, looking around.

This hallway was the mirror image of the other. Same gloomy carpet, same creepy wallpaper, same candles in brass holders.

Michael went back through to Dee's side. "Look— the candles even have the exact same drops of wax running down. It really is the *same* hallway, not just another one like it."

No matter how many times they went back and forth over the threshold, they kept getting the hallway.

"For some reason it's not letting us into your nightmare," Jenny said. "We just keep getting bounced back here."

"Oh, *too bad,*" said Michael. "I'm really going to miss facing it."

"All right, let me see this." Dee finally went through, the door swinging shut behind her. "Yep, same place," she said, looking around. "Like a revolving door to hell."

"Wasn't it Sartre who said hell was eternity spent in a room with your friends?" Michael asked grandly.

"Oh, quit showing off your A in world literature," said Jenny. "Unless—was *that* your nightmare, Mike?"

Michael deflated a bit. "Uh, actually, no. Mine was more of a kid thing, really."

"But what was it?"

Michael seemed to be blushing. Scratching under the collar of his gray sweatshirt, he shook his head.

"'Each of you has a secret you would rather die than reveal. . . .'" Dee quoted portentously from the game card. "I'll bet it was something *really* embarrassing, like the potty monster, huh, Mikey?" As she spoke she turned the doorknob. It wouldn't budge. "Oh, great, it's locked again."

"If we're stuck here again, we might as well sit down," Audrey said.

There didn't seem to be anything else to do. They sat, and Michael talked. One thing you could always count on, Jenny thought—that Michael wouldn't run out of things to talk about.

"When I think," said Michael, "that I could have stayed home and watched 'Ren and Stimpy' tonight . . ."

"This isn't much of a game. No reset. It's win, lose, or die," Michael said.

"You heard the one about the bunny and the hair dryer?" he said.

"Michael," Audrey said scathingly.

While he was talking, Michael had taken off one of his battered tennis shoes. It had a hole in the toe. Audrey stared in genteel horror at his limp sock on the floor.

"I can't help it—I've got an itch. Ah . . . that's better," Michael said, scratching vigorously. "So what'd you say to—that guy—after we all got whooshed out of the parlor?" he said to Jenny. "I mean—" He fumbled for words as all three girls looked at him. "I mean—it was pretty obvious what he wanted—and you said he kept you there alone—"

"Whatever he wants," Jenny said shortly, "he's not getting it."

"Of course not," Audrey huffed. "What an idea."

"She wouldn't give him the time of day," Dee said curtly.

"I don't even know what he sees in me," Jenny said.

The others all looked at each other. Then Dee snorted. "No, you wouldn't, would you? But everybody else does. Except Zach, probably, but then he's your cousin."

"It's not just looks," Audrey said. "You're *good.*
Too good, sometimes. I've told you—"

"Aba would say your soul is straight," Dee interrupted.

"Just like a Girl Scout," Michael said helpfully.
"Sweet and simple and honest."

"But he's *bad,*" Jenny said.

"That's the point," Dee said. "Badness always
wants goodness."

"And opposites attract," Audrey said grimly.
"Look at Michael and me."

Michael said hastily, "So who do you think he is,
anyway?"

"I think he's a Visitor," Dee said, to Jenny's
surprise. "You know, an alien that abducts people."

Michael stared, scratching his chin. Audrey
frowned.

"Don't be ridiculous," she said. "He's no alien—
just look at him. And where's his spaceship?"

"I think he can look like whatever he wants to,"
Dee said, scratching her arm. "And maybe they don't
really need spaceships. He's taken us to another
planet, hasn't he?"

"Another *world,* maybe. There's a difference,"
Audrey shot back. "And according to him he did it
with a rune. Which makes him—"

"What? The Erlking? I don't think so, dear. You're
just saying that because it's what you're most afraid
of."

"And Visitors are what you're most afraid of,
dear," Audrey said, working her perfect nails over
her palm. It was turning into a vintage Dee-Audrey
feud.

"Girls, girls," Michael said. "Personally, I think he's a demon. Jenny's demon lover." He smiled ingenuously, digging under his collar again. Dee and Audrey both glared. Jenny just felt a chill deep inside.

"Look, I believe in demons," Michael said. "Why shouldn't they exist? And if they *do* exist, that guy has gotta be one."

Throughout this conversation Jenny had gradually become aware of a discomfort. The skin on her arm was tingling—no, itching. She scratched at it absently, but the itching got worse. And worse. She looked down.

Even in the dim light she could see the mark on her arm. A dark spot, like a strawberry birthmark. But she didn't have any birthmarks. And this spot wasn't strawberry-colored . . .

. . . it was green.

At the same moment Michael, who'd thrust one hand inside his sleeve to scratch his arm, made a strange sound. His eyes bulged, his expression changed. He shoved the sweatshirt sleeve up.

Jenny gasped.

There was something growing on his arm.

A plant. There were leaves, fresh and green and young, looking like newly sprouted mint, growing from his flesh.

The next instant they were all on their feet, looking at themselves in the candlelight. Each of them was growing patches of green. Jenny's were like moss, Audrey's like mold.

Jenny gulped. Like Dee and Audrey, she was horrified. But Michael went hysterical.

"Get it off me! *Get it off!*" He thrust his arm out blindly at Jenny.

Even gritting her teeth, she couldn't bring herself to touch the sprigs. Dee took hold of one and pulled.

"Ow!" Michael yelled. Dee stopped. "No, go on! I don't care how much it hurts. Pull it out!"

Dee pulled harder. The plant hung on. Jenny could just glimpse a network of thin roots like white threads connecting it to his arm. Blood began to ooze out of several pores as Dee kept pulling.

Michael was screaming.

Finally Dee swallowed, her nostrils flared.

"Mike, I can't keep pulling. I can't. It's taking your skin with it."

"I don't care! I don't care!" Michael still wouldn't open his eyes. He grabbed at the plants himself with his other hand. Jenny pressed a hand to her mouth to stop from gasping.

Sprigs were growing on his other hand, too. Growing even more luxuriantly than on the first.

"Mike, it's . . . it's all over you," she whispered.

Michael's eyes flew open, and he looked at his hands. "Oh, God. Oh, GodGodGod . . ."

In one frenzied motion he yanked his sweatshirt over his head, pulling his arms out. His chest and stomach were thickly covered with new leaves. They stirred with his breath, brushing one another lightly.

Michael's screams rang from the ceiling.

"Chill out!" Dee finally got him in a choke hold, preventing him from running raving down the hall. His eyes were wild and set, and he was breathing like a lathered horse.

"We've got to do something for him," Jenny said. She could hardly bear the moss on her forearm, but she had to forget about that. Michael was so much worse off.

"Yeah—but what?" Dee was trying to keep Michael under control. He seemed about to go into convulsions, clawing at himself.

Audrey stepped forward. Jenny guessed that she was actually more upset by the growths than anyone but Michael—appearance meant a lot to Audrey. But Audrey had herself in iron control.

"Michael Allen Cohen, look at me!" she rapped out.

He turned wild dark eyes on her.

"You calm down *now*. Understand? *Verstehen Sie?*"

A glimmer of sanity showed in Michael's eyes.

"Right *now*," Audrey said severely, and putting her palms on either side of his face, she kissed him.

When she backed up, Michael had cherry lipstick all over his mouth. He looked a lot calmer.

"I live to obey," he said weakly.

"You live to kibitz," said Audrey.

"We've all got to stay calm," Jenny said. "We've got to *think*. How can we get rid of these things? We can't pull them out. So what else can we do?"

"Weed-killer," Dee muttered. There was some exotic red-and-green-leafed plant growing on her, almost harmonizing with her dark skin.

"We don't have *anything* here to work with," Audrey said. "Never mind anything deadly to plants."

Michael spoke up in a whisper—but a whisper with a new note in it.

"We've got fire."

Jenny looked up at the candle in its brass holder.

"You can let go of me, now," Michael told Dee. "I won't go anywhere. I want to see if that candle will come out."

Dee released him. He tried to take a step, then stopped. He squatted down to stare, his head almost at floor level. Jenny bent, too.

His bare foot was rooted to the floor by a mat of white tendrils.

They were growing out of his sole and into the black carpet. He could barely raise his foot an inch, and only by turning it sideways could he see the roots.

As Jenny slowly looked up, she expected him to go frantic again. But Audrey reached out and firmly took his hand, her fingers crushing the leaves on the back.

Michael was shaking, but he stayed rational.

"Get the candle," he said thickly.

Dee lifted it out easily. "I'm going to try it on myself first," she said.

"No. Me."

Dee slanted a sloe-eyed look at him, then nodded. She tilted the candle to apply the flame to a leaf on his arm.

The leaf seemed to melt slightly in a crescent where the flame touched it. There was a bad smell as the edge blackened. Nothing else happened.

"Try the roots."

Dee tried lower, very close to Michael's skin. Michael flinched away from the heat, but Audrey held him steady.

The plant started to shrivel.

"That's it!"

"Can you stand it?" Dee asked.

"I can stand anything to get these off. With the right kind of incentive, of course." He looked hopefully at Audrey, who was still holding him and murmuring encouragement.

Jenny smiled to herself. To be inane and lecherous when you're scared to death required a special kind of bravery.

Dee burned more roots. The plants began to drop off more and more quickly, shriveling at the first touch of the flame.

Michael was almost sobbing in relief. His arms and torso were clear.

"Anything—ah, lower?" Dee gestured with the candle at Michael's sweatpants.

"No! And watch where you're waving that thing. I plan to be a family man."

"Look," Jenny said softly.

The patch of moss on her skin was getting smaller and smaller. In a moment it had faded altogether. The same was happening to Dee and Audrey. Michael's feet came free of the floor.

And then they were all laughing, admiring their clear, perfect skin, touching it, holding it up to the others. Just exactly like the scene at the end of *Ben Hur*, Jenny thought, where the two women are miraculously cured of leprosy. Michael put his sweatshirt back on and kissed Audrey once more.

"You had some mold on your lips before," he said. "I didn't like to mention it."

"No, you didn't, Aud," Dee muttered in Audrey's ear. Audrey looked helplessly at Mike, but with some indulgence.

"So this *was* your nightmare, and we got through it," Jenny said. "This hallway is your nightmare room. Which means that if we go back through that door . . ."

The door opened under Dee's hand. They walked through into the hallway, apparently the same hallway they had just left. But with two differences, Jenny noticed. In this hallway there was no candle missing from the bracket. And there was a scrap of white paper on the floor.

A picture of a huge green plant, something on the order of a rubber plant, with arms and legs sticking out. No head.

"Ugh," Jenny said.

"My nightmare," Michael said, still looking embarrassed. "Turning into a plant. It's so stupid—I think it came from this book I read when I was in third grade. It had a story about a kid who was so dirty that things started to grow on her—little radishes and veggies. And it just freaked me out. I mean, it was this harmless story, but for some reason I just flipped. I kept thinking about that kid, all crusted with dirt, with green stuff sprouting from her—it made me sick."

"You're making *me* sick," Audrey said.

"And then the parents pulled them—the veggies —they pulled them off her—"

"Stop it," Dee commanded.

"Like I said, it was stupid, a kid's thing."

"I don't think it was stupid, I think it was *horrible*. And I think you were smart and brave, the way you dealt with it," Jenny said. Michael's soulful eyes widened at the unprecedented compliments, and he gave her a rumpled grin.

The unseen clock struck one. There was something

eerie about the way it echoed. Morning is coming, Jenny thought.

"We'd better get moving," Dee said, just as Michael made a stifled sound.

"What's wrong—" Audrey began, but then she saw it, too, in the darkness of the hall where nothing had been before.

A staircase.

10

Excitement bubbled up in Jenny. "Finally we can *go* somewhere."

"And get out of this freaking hallway," Dee said.

Michael was looking awed. "It's just like going up to the next level of a video game."

But Audrey pursed her lips. When Jenny asked why, Audrey gave her a sideways glance under spiky dark lashes.

"One thing about video games—the farther you go, the harder they get," she said. *"N'est-ce pas?"*

The stairs had rubber padding with the ridges worn almost to nothing. Jenny couldn't see the top from where she stood—the roof of the Haunted Mansion hall was in the way.

"What are we waiting for?" Dee said and vaulted onto the steps. Then she grabbed for the railing—as soon as her foot touched a step, the whole staircase had started moving with a jerk. It was a wheezing, groaning, shivering escalator.

"Oh, geez," Michael said. "I hate to tell you this, but when I was a kid I was scared of escalators. I was afraid they might catch the end of my muffler or something—"

"You don't wear mufflers," Audrey said and shoved him on.

"Mike, if you're scared of escalators, then this one is probably your fault," Jenny said, stepping on behind him. "Remember, he gets it all from us."

As they neared the top, Jenny found they were riding directly toward a mirror. In fact, she discovered when she looked down the hall—after helping Mike jump off the escalator at the strategic moment —there were mirrors everywhere.

The hallway downstairs had been dark—this one was exactly the opposite. Light bounced and rainbowed off the mirrors lining the zigzagging walls until Jenny saw colored streaks even with her eyes closed. In fact, the mirrored walls zigged and zagged so sharply that it was impossible to get a clear view for more than a few feet. You had to veer alternately right and left to follow the hallway's path, and anything in the bend before you or behind you was invisible.

"All right, who put *these* here?" Dee demanded.

"Are my legs really that short? Or are these trick mirrors?" Audrey asked, pivoting.

Michael made one effort to straighten his wrinkled gray sweats and then gave up.

Jenny's own reflection made her uncomfortable. She seemed to hear Julian's voice in her mind: *"Eyes as green as cypress and hair like liquid amber. . . ."*

That wasn't what she saw. Just now Jenny saw a girl with flushed cheeks, whose hair was clinging to her forehead in little damp curls, whose tissue-linen blouse was beginning to go limp, and whose flowing cotton skirt was dusty and grass-stained.

"Right or left—take your pick," she said, glancing up and down the hallway.

"Left," Dee said firmly, and they went that way, zigging and zagging with the acute turns.

The mirrors were disconcerting. Everywhere Jenny looked her image was thrown back at her, and thrown from mirror to mirror so that she saw herself coming and going, reflected to infinity on all sides. Stay in this place long enough and you might forget which one is really you, she thought.

As in the other hallway, there were no deviations from the pattern, nothing to distinguish any part of it from any other. It was especially nerve-racking not being able to see more than one turn behind you, and not knowing what might be waiting around the next turn ahead. Images of the Creeper and the Lurker went through Jenny's mind.

"Dee, slow *down,*" Jenny said as Dee's long, light step took her out of sight for the third time. Dee was navigating the corridor like a skier on a slalom, plunging in and out of the sharp turns, while the rest of them walked with hands outstretched to help them tell reflection from reality.

"No, you guys hurry *up*—" Dee's voice was responding from the next bend, and then there was a flash.

It seemed to reflect from everywhere at once, but Jenny thought it came from ahead. She and Audrey and Michael stood frozen for a moment, then hurried forward.

Dee was standing, hands on her hips, in front of a

door. It was mirrored like the walls, but Jenny figured it *had* to be a door because there was a red button like an elevator button beside it. When she looked hard she could distinguish the door's outline from the mirror around it.

Above the red button was a blue light bulb, round as a clown's nose.

"It just appeared," Dee said and snapped her fingers. "Like *that*. In that flash."

From the turn ahead they heard whimpering.

"Summer!" Jenny, Dee, and Audrey exclaimed simultaneously.

It was Summer, huddled in the next bend, her spun-sugar curls resting on her folded arms, her legs drawn beneath her china blue shirtdress. She looked up with a little hysterical cry at their approach.

"Is it really you?"

"Yes," Jenny said, kneeling. She was a little frightened by the expression in Summer's eyes.

"Really, really you?"

"Yes. Oh, Summer." Worriedly, Jenny put her arms around the smaller girl and felt her trembling.

"I've been alone here so long, and I kept seeing myself, and then sometimes I thought I saw other people, but when I ran toward them they weren't there. . . ."

"Who have you seen?" Jenny asked.

"Sometimes Zachary—and sometimes *him*. He *scares* me, Jenny." Summer buried her small face in Jenny's vest.

He scares me, too, Jenny thought. She said, "There's nothing to be frightened of now. We're really here. See?"

Summer managed a watery smile.

135

"Poor sun bunny," Michael said. "I guess it must be your nightmare next."

"Good job, Mr. Tactful," Dee said under her breath.

They explained about the nightmares to Summer. She wasn't as disturbed as Jenny thought she might be.

"Anything to get out of *here,*" she said.

"I know. I've only been here twenty minutes, and I hate the place already," Dee said. "Anybody for claustrophobia?"

In front of the door Jenny hesitated with her finger on the button. "I don't suppose you want to tell us what you drew for your nightmare," she said. She didn't have much hope; none of the others had told.

"Okay," Summer said readily. "It was a messy room."

"A messy *room?*" Michael said. "Oh, horror."

"No, really, Summer," Audrey said with a briskly adult air. "It'll help if you tell us."

Dee flashed an amused ebony glance at her.

"I did tell you. It's a messy room."

"It's all right, Summer," Jenny said gently. "We'll deal with it when we get there." She pushed the red button. The blue light went on. The door slid open.

It was a messy room.

"You see," Summer said.

It was Summer's bedroom, only more so. Ever since Jenny had known Summer, her room had been messy. Summer's parents were refugees from the sixties, and everything in their house was slightly frayed or weathered, but as Michael said, Summer herself had clutter down to a fine art. When you

visited her you usually couldn't see the handmade
tie-dyed curtains at the window or the bright patch-
work quilt on the bed, because of the things hanging
from them or piled up in front of them or scattered
on top of them.

In the room behind the mirrored door, Jenny
couldn't even see the *bed*. There was a small clear
space in front of the closet—everything else was
obscured by piles of junk.

Dee and Michael were giggling. "Trust you, Sunshine, to have a nightmare like this," Dee said.

Jenny sighed, not nearly as amused. "All right,
everybody, let's go in. I suppose we have to clean it
up—there must be a door somewhere along one of
the far walls."

"Hey, wait. I don't do the C-word," Michael
protested, alarmed. "Besides, dust is bad for my
allergies."

"In," said Audrey, taking him by the ear.

They all squeezed in between the closet and the
piles. The door slid noiselessly shut behind them—
and disappeared.

"Talk about claustrophobia," Michael gasped.

"Cette chambre est une vrai pagaille," Audrey said
under her breath.

"What?" Jenny asked.

"I said this is one messy room. Summer, how can
you stand it?"

Summer's delft-blue eyes filled with tears. "My
real room isn't as bad as *this*. This is my nightmare,
dummy!"

"Well, why this kind of nightmare?" Audrey said,
not softening.

"Because my mom never yells about my room, but once my nana came to visit, and she almost passed out. I still dream about what she said."

"Don't make her feel bad," Jenny whispered to Audrey. "Try to clear a path around the edges," she said aloud, "and check every wall for the door."

The piles of junk were amazingly varied. There were heaps of rumpled clothes, year-old magazines, disjointed Ray-Bans, spindled cassette tapes, unstrung string bikinis, crushed frozen yogurt cups, bent photographs, mismatched sandals, dry felt-tip pens, chewed pencils, twisted headphones, musty towels, endless mounds of underwear, and a zoo of bedraggled stuffed animals. Also a dog-chewed Frisbee, a mashed Twister mat, and a futon that smelled like somebody's bottom.

"It's spider city here," Dee said, gathering up one of the heaps. "Haven't you ever heard of Raid?"

"I believe in live and let live," Summer said vaguely.

It really *was* a nightmare of sorts, Jenny thought—a nightmare of tedium. But Dee worked with tireless energy and Audrey with fastidious precision, and slowly they forged a path through the debris. Michael was no good at all—he stopped to leaf through every magazine he picked up.

They were getting to a different type of garbage—a type that made Audrey wrinkle up her nose. Blackened avocado husks, mildewed newspapers, and plastic glasses with the dregs of unidentifiable liquids in them.

Then Jenny lifted a box of odds and ends and saw something like a pressed flower on the hardwood floor underneath. But it wasn't a flower, it was the wrong shape. At first she didn't recognize it, then she saw the little muzzle and the tiny curled-up feet. It was a flat and desiccated mouse.

She couldn't help gasping.

I can't touch that, I can't, I *can't*.

Dee scraped it up with a 1991 calendar and threw it in the closet. Jenny felt a whisper of terror inside her, unease that went beyond disgust at the mouse.

The garbage got worse and worse—like what you'd find at a dump, nothing that would be in anybody's bedroom. Food in all stages of decomposition. Every kind of refuse, trash, and litter.

No one was smiling anymore.

Dee picked up a tattered Easter basket, paused. An *awful* smell wafted from it. She stirred the cellophane grass with one long finger, and then her face convulsed. In the basket was a solid mass of white, writhing maggots.

"God!" In one fluid motion Dee threw the basket at the closet, where it hit the door and scattered a shower of white. Michael bolted up from his magazine with a yell. Audrey and Summer were shrieking.

Jenny felt the quick, cold touch of real fear.

"Summer—just *what* did your grandmother say about your room?" she said.

"Oh—she said things were growing in it," Summer reported, her eyes large and worried. "She said it would attract bugs. She said it looked like an earthquake hit it. She said someday I would get lost in it and never come out."

Dee, who had been staring at Summer, now cut a glance of startled revelation at Jenny. "Uh-*huh*," she said.

The tension in the room was palpable.

"And just what kind of nightmares do you have about it?" Jenny asked, trying to discipline her voice.

"Oh." Summer shivered. "Well—it's like I hear a scratchy noise, and then I look and it's these cockroaches—but they're big, big as . . . as sneakers. And then I see this thing on the floor. It's like fungus, sort of a column of fungus, but it's got a kind of mouth on the top and it's howling. It's howling fungus."

Summer's lips were trembling by now.

"It may not sound scary, but it was. It was the scariest thing I've ever seen in my life."

A primitive warning was going off in Jenny's brain. She, Audrey, Dee, and Michael all looked at one another. "It sounds plenty scary to me," she said. "I think maybe we'd better get moving."

Michael's lips were puckered in a soundless whistle. "I think maybe you're right," he muttered. He bent to work without another word of complaint.

The closet was full by now, and they were just transferring things from before them to behind them, like digging a tunnel. The garbage kept getting grosser and grosser and scarier and scarier. Things Jenny didn't want to touch with her hands. She wore crumpled T-shirts like oven mitts to move them.

Then the bugs came.

It started with a rustle, a pleasant sound like a taffeta prom dress. Jenny stiffened, then turned slowly to look.

A cockroach, flat and brown. But it was huge, far larger than Jenny's foot. It crawled languidly out of the floor vent, squirming through somehow, its barbed back legs catching on the metal louvers. Its feet made soft ticking sounds on the paper debris.

Summer gave a reedy shriek and pointed at it. Then another one came out of the vent, and another. Summer's pointing finger became a shaky blur.

Jenny reached for a water glass to revive her and snatched her hand back. The glass was jam-packed with crickets, antennae twitching delicately.

Summer saw it. She stopped pointing and went still.

Smaller roaches emerged from a discarded candy box, the frilly paper cups crinkling as the bugs crept out.

Summer's face was so white there were blue patches under her eyes.

Iridescent green beetles the size of footballs began to climb the walls. They flexed their chitinous outer wings, their membranous inner wings hanging out like dragging petticoats.

Summer stood like a statue of ice.

Jenny looked up. A dozen brown moths as big as small kites were clinging flat to the ceiling, their dark-spotted wings outstretched.

"Come on, Summer, *help* us!" Audrey said in a fear-clotted voice as she raked at the trash. Disturbed ants swarmed out of it, forming thick trails like black waterfalls over the debris.

Summer didn't move. She was staring at one of the hard-shelled beetles like a witless rabbit caught in a headlight.

The ground rocked beneath Jenny's feet.

At first she thought it was some effect of the garbage shifting. Then she remembered: *"She said it looked like an earthquake hit it. . . ."*

"We have to hurry!" she shouted at the same time as Dee yelled, "Go, go!"

141

They were clawing through the garbage now, tearing just enough away from the wall to reveal cracked and peeling wallpaper, to make sure there was no door. They climbed on the smaller mounds, wading through them.

The ground shook again.

The whisper of terror inside Jenny had become a scream.

"Hurry," she gasped, clearing refuse with sweeps of her arms. "Hurry, hurry . . ."

The towering piles of rubbish quaked.

They were all working frenetically, even Michael. Only Summer stood rooted in horror.

"The door!" Dee shouted, from the top of a pile.

Jenny's head snapped up. Relief flooded through her. Barely visible above a stinking pile she could see the rectangular molding of the door.

"It opens *in,*" Audrey said. "We have to get all this stuff out of the way."

They scrambled over each other, ripping at the pile. A cockroach climbed onto Jenny's foot; she kicked it off. Time to scream later.

The room shook again. Jenny looked up and her breath hissed in. There were ominous cracks in the ceiling.

At that moment Dee and Michael cleared the last rubble from the door.

With a thankful sob Jenny helped them pull it open.

Then she turned to look back.

What she saw wasn't anybody's *room.* It was Hell. There were huge cracks in the floor with monstrous, mutant bugs crawling out. The ceiling was buckling and plaster was filtering down. The moths, disturbed, were fluttering through the air, their wings making a sound like huge cards shuffling. And sprouting like grotesque anemones among the refuse were objects Jenny didn't recognize. They looked like drooping sea cucumbers and they were green-gray.

Audrey and Michael had stumbled out into the hall of mirrors. Dee was holding the door. The earth rumbled again.

"Summer, come on!" Jenny shouted.

Summer turned toward her voice, her large blue eyes blind. She took a step toward Jenny.

One of the growths directly in her path straightened up. It became a column. At the top of the column there was an aperture that flared open and shut.

The aperture opened wide. A demented, obscene sound came out.

It was howling.

The other growths were straightening. The moaning siren sound doubled, tripled. They were between Summer and the door.

Summer turned and stumbled back toward the closet, shrieking.

"Summer, *no!* Come back!"

The ground heaved. The piles of garbage were toppling, falling into the clear path. The mutant bugs skittered around in a frenzy. They seemed to be heading toward Summer. The fungus howled.

Summer's shrieks gave way to full-throated screaming.

"Summer!" Adrenaline kicked in and Jenny plunged into the garbage, trying to climb it.

"Jenny, come back!" Dee shouted. More rubbish

fell. Jenny couldn't see Summer at all. The screams were fading.

"Jenny, I can't hold the door!"

The screams fell silent. Only the howling went on. *"Summer!"*

The earth jerked violently.

"It's coming down!" Dee shouted, and Jenny felt a hand grab her, pull her backward.

"No—we have to get Summer!"

"We can't get anybody! Come on!"

"No—*Summer!*" Jenny screamed, turning again.

Dee ducked and caught Jenny around the waist. Jenny found herself flying over Dee's shoulders, out the door.

Michael and Audrey grabbed her. Through the open door Jenny saw the ceiling come down. Dee staggered out and fell beside them. Jenny didn't have the strength to stand up.

Then the door slammed shut as the toppling piles fell against it.

"Look," Michael said in a thick voice.

The door was disappearing.

It did a slow fade, like a still frame in a movie. It was a door, it was a slightly misty door, it was a transparent door with mirror showing through, it was a mirrored wall.

Jenny was staring wildly at her own image.

She could see the others in the mirror. Audrey was white as china. Dee's face was gray. Michael looked numb. They huddled on the carpet, stunned.

It had happened with such terrible suddenness.

Jenny whispered, "When Dee was late coming out of Audrey's nightmare, the door didn't disappear. It stayed there—and she came out. But this time . . ."

"God," said Dee in a very low voice.

There was a long silence. Audrey, finally, was the one to say the words.

"She's dead."

Jenny put her face in her hands. It was a gesture she would never have thought she'd use. At the moment it just happened. She wanted to hide from the world. She wanted to make everything that had happened unhappen.

"It's not fair," she whispered. "She never hurt anybody." Then she was standing, shouting to the echoing hallway. "It's not fair. It's not *fair,* damn you! She didn't deserve it! It's not *fair!*"

"Jenny. Jenny, calm down—come on, now. Jenny, please—just sit down, okay?"

They were all trying to hold her. Jenny realized she wasn't in control of herself. She was trembling violently, and her throat hurt from screaming.

As suddenly as it had come, the hysterical energy faded. Jenny felt herself falling.

They set her down.

"It's okay," Dee said, and Jenny felt a hand stroking her hair. At any other time it would have surprised her. Now she felt nothing. "It's okay to be upset," Dee said.

They didn't understand. It was Jenny's fault. She was the one who had gotten them into this. If she had kissed Julian in the Erlking's cavern, she could have gotten Summer out.

As if to mock her, an unseen clock struck two. But Jenny could only sit.

11

What's taking them so long?" Dee said.

Audrey and Michael had gone off to see if they could find Zach, who they figured must be around here somewhere. Or if they could find water—or a blanket—or *something*—for Jenny.

Jenny was in bad shape. She was slumped against the slanting mirrored wall opposite Summer's door —what had been Summer's door. There wasn't a trace of the exit from Summer's nightmare left, but Jenny wouldn't leave this place.

Jenny ached. All she could think of, in between waves of grayness, was Summer. Summer had joined their group in fourth grade, after she, Tom, Dee, Zach, and Michael were already friends. Tiny, muddled, and very sweet, Summer had needed to be taken care of, and taking care was what Jenny did best.

But not this time. This time Jenny had screwed up. And Summer was gone.

146

Jenny still didn't believe it had really happened. Summer would come walking out of that mirror any second now, all thistledown hair and dark blue eyes. Any second now.

Summer didn't.

Jenny let her head drop back against the wall.

"I'm going to look for them," Dee said. "They've been too long, they might be in trouble. You stay here, okay? Promise you'll stay right here." Her voice was slow and clear, the voice you'd use to talk to a child.

Eyes shut, Jenny made some slight motion with her head.

"Okay. I'll be back in a minute."

Jenny's mind drifted back into a haze. Summer climbing a tree at camp, Summer at Newport Beach falling off a surfboard, Summer at school chewing on a pencil. Summer laughing, Summer puzzled, Summer's blue eyes filled with tears.

She didn't have a mean bone in her body, Jenny thought. She was a *good* person. Something like this can't happen to a *good* person.

Can it?

She saw the flash even through closed lids.

Summer! she thought, opening her eyes. But the mirror in front of her showed only her own pale, anxious face and disarrayed hair.

Maybe it had come from the side. Which way? On her feet, Jenny looked to the right and left, dazzled by the multiple reflections. She didn't even know which way Dee had gone.

She went right, veering back and forth around the zigzag mirrors.

Turning a corner, she saw dozens of reflections of a round blue light bulb.

She caught her breath sharply. The blue light was on, the red button beneath it was depressed. Beside it was a dark rectangle—an open door.

Numb to caution, Jenny poked her head in. She could see only darkness inside. None of the light from the hallway seemed to penetrate.

Had Audrey and Michael gone in here? Had Dee? Could Summer—

With a click the button popped out, the door began to close. Jenny had an instant to choose: jump back or jump forward. She jumped forward.

The door slid noiselessly shut behind her, and she stared around, trying to see in the gloom. She could make out shapes like a row of shelves, something on a tripod, a tall lamp. Then she knew where she was. It was dim simply because the lights were off.

As her eyes adjusted she recognized a giant mural print on one wall. It showed cafeteria tables stacked in a glorious pyramid, one trash can on each end at each level—a marvel of engineering. Jenny knew that picture well. She, Tom, and Dee had spent an entire night stacking those tables and listening to Zach's imperious demands for "one more shot." It had been one of the more hysterical and terrifying adventures of their sophomore year.

This was her cousin Zach's garage, converted into a studio. It felt almost like home—but there was no one in sight.

The darkroom, Jenny thought, and followed the special L-shaped hallway Zach had built—a light trap, he called it—to the little room nestled within the garage. She pushed aside the curtain at the entrance.

The amber safe light shone on a single figure's back, on a flannel shirt and a casual ponytail.

"Zach!" Jenny ran to him, but he didn't turn around. "Zach, it's me, Jenny. Zach—what are you *doing?*"

He was gently rocking a tray full of chemicals with a print in it. His body was stiff and resistant, but Jenny turned him by force. Even in this light she could see he looked—tranced. The look she'd seen first in the living room when he'd insisted on turning more game cards, and then in the parlor when all the rest of them were freaking out.

"Oh, Zach, what's wrong with you?" she said and threw her arms around him. She'd been worried about him all night; she'd been planning to comfort him, to help. But now she didn't have the strength. She desperately needed help herself.

He scarcely seemed to notice she was there. He pushed her away and turned back to agitating the tray.

"Zachary, did Dee come in here? Have you seen Audrey or Michael?"

His voice was slow, dragging, but matter-of-fact.

"I haven't seen anybody. I was sitting out there. Where the mirrors are. Then I saw a flashgun go off. When I looked for it, I found a door. I pushed the button and went in."

A flashgun—of course, that was how Zach would interpret the bursts of light in the hallway. "But what are you *doing?*" Jenny said.

"It was all set up for me. The print was already in

149

the developer." Somewhere a timer went off, and he pulled away from Jenny's reaching hand. "I have to rinse it now."

Jenny blinked painfully as he turned the white light on. She watched his careful, clever fingers as he rinsed the print and plastered it wetly against the wall, standing back to evaluate it, frowning.

"Zach, *please*. You have to listen." The numbness over Summer was wearing off. Zach was her blood relative, and right here, and in trouble. In this light she could see how pale his narrow face was. She could also see the fixed look in his clear gray eyes. "Don't you realize this is your nightmare? We can't waste time—we have to find a door to get out. *Zach!*"

He pushed her away again. "I have to finish this job. I have to . . ."

She was barely in time to catch him as he collapsed. But when she did he didn't push her away again. He clung to her like a frightened child.

"Jenny . . . sorry . . ."

"It's okay." She held him tightly, almost rocking him. "It's okay, I'm here. That's what cousins are for."

After a minute he tried to straighten up, but she still held him, encouraging him to hold her back. She needed comfort as much as he did, and Zach had always been there for her. Before their families had moved out to California, she and Zach had lived next door to each other. They'd played Indians in the cherry orchard behind their houses. That was in the days before Zach decided he liked photographs better than people, when Zach's gray eyes had been warm instead of winter-cool.

Her cousin's mind was obviously following the same track. "Just like when we were kids," he said with what was probably supposed to be a laugh.

"And you'd get all scraped up climbing trees, and we'd wash you with the hose so Aunt Lil wouldn't get mad," Jenny said. She laughed, herself, muffled against Zach's shoulder. It was almost like crying. "Oh, Zach, I'm so glad I found you."

"Me, too." He sighed. "I've been feeling pretty weird."

"Everything's been awful," Jenny said, and once again her voice was shaking badly. "I've been so scared—and now . . ."

She couldn't bring herself to mention Summer. The words stuck in her throat.

"It's okay," he said. "We're together now. We'll make things okay."

A hose and a Band-Aid aren't going to help this time, Jenny thought, but it was easier just to hold on to Zach. Tighter and tighter. Exchanging comfort without words. He was stroking her hair and it felt good—soothing. She seemed to feel strength flowing from his body to hers.

And something else. A warmth that surprised her. Zach was usually so cool. Now he was holding her and caressing her almost as if she were some toddler that needed pacifying.

Or—as if he weren't her cousin, but her boyfriend.

She pushed the thought away. Zach was just being kind. He wanted to help—and he was helping. She felt better, simply absorbing his sympathy, his affection. His—tenderness.

She leaned against him, letting him support her weight. Feeling secure. Cared for. Safe.

When he kissed the back of her neck, it was so tenderly it didn't disturb the safe feeling. Zach was nice. She loved him; she was happy to know he loved her.

When he kissed her again, an unexpected tremor ran through her.

Now—she wasn't supposed to feel like *that*. Not with Zach. He shouldn't—he really shouldn't. . . .

But she didn't want to pull away from him or spoil the moment.

His lips were warm on the back of her neck. A shock of sweetness passed through Jenny, this time too strong to be ignored. That felt—she *knew* she mustn't feel that way. Her hands went up to his arms, to push at him.

"Zach," she whispered. "I think we're both—a little upset. We're not ourselves."

"I know," Zach said, as if it hurt him. "I'm sorry—I . . ." He straightened, loosening his grip a little, but then he kissed her hair. She felt his lips moving, felt his warm breath there.

"Zachary," she said. "It's *wrong*. We're cousins." The problem was that although her words were strong, her voice wasn't. She could barely breathe. And she didn't move away.

"Half cousins," he said. It was true, although Jenny seldom thought of it—her mother and his were only half sisters. "And besides, I can't help it. I can't help it." His kisses were coming faster.

His urgency caught Jenny in a rush of elemental feeling. She kept thinking, *but there's something else*—without remembering what the something was. Then she whispered, "But, Tom . . ."—and shock swept over her.

She hadn't thought about Tom since—since—
She couldn't remember when.

Zach was saying that he couldn't help Tom, either.

"He doesn't deserve you." The words came on a warm wave of breath in her ear. "He doesn't love you enough. I was always afraid to say it, but you know it's true."

Despite his slimness Zach's muscles were hard against her. Jenny tried to protest, but the words caught in her throat.

"And now I know you don't love him enough, either. You weren't meant to be with him." Zach's voice was soft and reasonable, his words running together in a velvet sound.

Then he was looking down at her. A clear light seemed to shine through his intense face. His winter-gray eyes looked almost pale blue.

"You can't fight something like this, Jenny," he whispered. "You know you can't."

Jenny shut her eyes and turned her face up.

He kissed her and her senses reeled.

They seemed to melt together. Jenny felt herself sinking beneath his embrace. So soft . . . kissing had never been so soft before. She couldn't think anymore. She was flying. She was deep underwater.

Pure sensation overwhelmed her. She was kissing him back as she had never kissed Tom. His hair was loose under her fingers; it must have come out of the ponytail. She wanted to feel all of it. It was so much softer than she'd realized. She'd always thought of Zach as having rather coarse hair, but this was *so* soft . . . like silk or cat's fur under her fingertips. . . .

She heard the wild, whimpering sound she made,

and she knew, she *knew,* even as she was pulling back. Even as she was jerking away, she knew.

Julian's eyes were like liquid sapphires under sooty lashes. Heavy-lidded and dark with passion. He was wearing a plaid flannel shirt like Zach's shirt, stone-washed denims like Zach's denims, and running shoes like Zach's shoes. But he had a languid, careless grace Zach would never have. His hair looked bright as sand in moonlight.

Jenny was scrubbing her mouth with the back of her hand. A purely reflexive and senseless gesture. She was too shocked to be angry.

Did I know? Did I know underneath before he kissed me or while he was kissing me but before I pulled away did I know could I possibly have known . . . ?

She still couldn't make out what reality was.

"How could you know . . . ?" she whispered. "You acted like Zach—you knew things only he would know—"

"I've watched him," Julian said. "I've watched you. I'm the Shadow Man, Jenny—and I love you." His voice was soft, mesmerizing, and something inside Jenny began to melt at the very sound.

Then she thought of Summer.

Anger, hot and bright, surged through her and gave her strength. She looked into Julian's liquid-blue eyes. Any softness she'd ever had toward him had disappeared. She *hated* him now. Without a word she turned and walked out of the darkroom.

He followed her, flicking the garage lights on. He knew, of course, what she was thinking about.

"She agreed," he said. "Just like all the rest of you, she agreed to play the Game."

"She didn't know it was real!"

He quoted from the instructions. " 'I acknowledge that the Game is real. . . .' "

"You can talk all you want, Julian—but you killed her."

"I didn't do anything to her. Her own fear did that. She couldn't face her nightmare."

Jenny knew there was no point in arguing with him, but she couldn't help it. In a low, savage voice she said, "It wasn't fair."

He shook his head, looking almost amused. "Life isn't fair, Jenny. Haven't you learned that yet?"

Jenny was raging on. "What gives you the *right* to play with us this way? How can you *justify* it?"

"I don't need the right. Listen to me, Jenny. The worlds—all nine of them—are cruel. They don't care anything about you, or about *right.* There is no ultimate goodness. It's the law of the jungle. You don't need right—if you have strength."

"I don't believe you," Jenny said.

"That the world is cruel?" There was a newspaper on the bench; he picked it up. "Take a look at this and tell me that evil loses and good wins. Tell me that it's not the law of the jungle in your world."

Jenny didn't even want to look at the headlines. She'd seen too many in her life.

"Reality," Julian said, flashing a smile, "has teeth and claws. And since that's true, wouldn't you rather be one of the hunters than one of the hunted?"

Jenny shook her head. She had to admit the truth of what he was saying—about the world, at least. But she felt sick to her stomach.

"I'm offering you a choice," Julian said. His face had hardened. "I told you before that if I couldn't persuade you I would force you—somehow. If you won't agree I'll have to show you what I mean. I'm tired of playing, Jenny. I want this settled—one way or another."

"It is settled," Jenny said. "I'll never come to you. I *hate* you."

Anger flared like a twisting blue flame in Julian's eyes. "Don't you understand," he said, "that what happened to Summer can happen to you?"

Jenny felt a wave of coldness. "Yes," she said slowly. "I do."

And she did, at last. She probably wouldn't have believed it before. Wouldn't have believed Julian was capable of it, or that *she,* Jenny, could be vulnerable to it. Dying was for old people, not kids her age. Bad things—*really* bad things—didn't happen to good people.

But they did.

Now she knew that emotionally. In her heart. Sometimes bad things, the *worst,* happened to people who didn't deserve it at all. Even Summer. Even her.

Jenny felt as if she had learned some secret, been initiated into some worldwide club or community. The community of sorrow.

She was now one of the people who knew. Strangely, it gave her a sense of comfort to know that there were so many others, so many who'd had friends die, or lost parents, or had other terrible things happen that they never asked for.

There are a lot of us, she thought. Without realizing it, she'd begun to cry. We're everywhere. And we don't all turn hunter and take it out on other people. All of us don't.

Aba hadn't. Jenny suddenly remembered that Dee's grandmother had lost her husband in a racial incident. And she remembered something Aba had taped to her bathroom mirror, incongruous among all the glass and marble and gold fixtures. It was a handmade sign that said:

Do no harm.
Help when you can.
Return good for evil.

Jenny had never asked Aba about the sign. It didn't seem to need explaining.

Now she felt the community of sorrow strengthening her from all over. As if they were sympathizing, silently. Bad things—the worst—might happen to Jenny, right now. Jenny understood that.

She said, "You're right. Maybe things are that bad. But that doesn't mean I have to give in. I won't join you willingly, so you might as well try force."

"I will," he said.

It started so simply. Jenny heard a whining buzz and a bee landed on her sleeve.

It was just an ordinary bee, dusty-gold. It clung with its little feet to her tissue-linen blouse. But then she heard another buzz, and a second bee landed on her other sleeve.

Another buzz, and another.

Jenny hated bees. She was always the one at picnics shrieking, "Is there one in my hair?" She wanted to shoo these bees away, but she was afraid to provoke them.

She looked at Julian. At his wild, exotic sapphire

eyes and his beautifully sculpted face. At that moment, wearing Zach's lackluster clothing, his beauty was so unearthly it was frightening.

Another buzz and a bee *was* in her hair, its wings a blur of motion as it tangled and clung. She could see it in her peripheral vision.

Julian smiled.

Jenny heard a deeper sound, a *thrumming,* and she looked automatically for the source. A swarm of bees was clustered on one of the rafters of the garage, hanging down like some giant, pendulous fruit.

Jenny took a step backward and heard a warning *buzzzzz* from her hair. The ball of bees was moving, breaking up. Becoming a dark cloud.

Heading toward her.

Jenny looked once more at Julian, and then bees began to fall on her like hail. They clung to her arms, her shoulders, her breasts. She had to hold her arms away from her body in order to keep from crushing the ones on her sides. She knew that if she did that they would sting.

Then it simply became a nightmare, unreal.

They were heavy, covering her like a blanket. Too heavy. Jenny staggered. She shut her eyes because they were crawling out of her hair onto her face. She was inundated with bees, layer upon layer of them. They were clinging to each other now, because there was almost no part of her body clear of them. Her fingertips, some parts of her face. She felt their feet on her cheeks and wanted to scream, but she couldn't, she couldn't scream because if she did—if she did—

They'd get into her mouth. And then she'd lose her sanity. But she couldn't breathe well enough through her nose. Her chest was heaving and their weight was crushing her. She was going to have to open her mouth.

She was crying silently, trying not to move, to disturb them more than she could help. Julian's voice came to her.

"Just say the word, Jenny."

She could only shake her head slightly. The barest minimum of motion. But what she could manage, she did. She was still sobbing without a sound, terrified to move, but she would not—she *would not*—give in.

You can do whatever you like to me, she thought. In the dark beneath her bee-covered eyes she tried to hold on to consciousness, but it was like a thin thread slipping through her fingers. She grasped at it, felt it being snatched away from her.

She was fainting. Falling. But she wouldn't give in.

When I hit the ground and crush them, they'll go mad. They'll kill me, she thought.

But she never said the word to stop it.

She felt the darkness come as she began to fall.

12

Floating in gray dimness, she heard a clock strike three.

Wake up, she thought, but she didn't want to. She floated for a while again.

No, *wake up,* she thought. That's the alarm. You have to go to school . . . or something. You have to go see Zach.

Zach.

She was awake.

She was lying on the cold floor of her cousin's garage, chilled and stiff but bee-less. She looked at her hands and bare ankles. Not a mark. Julian hadn't let it happen.

But now she was stuck in a garage without a door. The light trap had only a curtain. All the other doors—the large one for cars and the regular one to the house—were simply missing, their spaces filled in with blank walls.

She had no idea what she was supposed to do next, and it was after three in the morning and she was tired.

Jenny looked at the corner of the studio where Zach took pictures. Zach's camera stood on a tripod. The tungsten floodlamp was turned on. The backdrop was a sheet of seamless paper from a roll maybe six feet wide. Zach had done a lot of photos by painting paper like that black and throwing handfuls of white flour at it. The result had looked a little like the Milky Way—white splashes on infinite space. Very strange and futuristic; Zach loved that kind of stuff.

This backdrop, though, had a door painted on it, too.

A knob protruded from the paper.

The way out, Jenny thought as she went over to it, but something inside her wasn't so sure. For some reason this black-and-white door made her chilled flesh creep.

What choice have you got? her mind asked simply.

She turned the knob. The door swung out. She stepped inside.

It was like being suspended among the stars. The door closed behind her, but Jenny scarcely noticed. The sky seemed very low, more like a ceiling. It was black with glowing white splotches. The ground was a velvety black dropcloth that went on forever in all directions.

It was awful, this sense of infinity all around, pulling at her. It reminded her of a dream she'd once had, where the ground stretched on endlessly, but the sky was close and solid overhead. Did Zach have the

161

same kind of dreams? Was this Zach's real nightmare?

The only landmarks in the limitless, featureless darkness were lamps—tungsten floodlamps like the ones Zach used. They formed little islands of brightness here and there, some white, some colored, fading out into the distance.

Jenny pivoted, trying to get her bearings—and drew in her breath sharply. The door was still behind her. It hadn't disappeared. She could walk right out again.

But if this was Zach's nightmare, he must be in here somewhere. She couldn't leave without looking for him.

After a moment's hesitation she headed for the nearest floodlamp, a neon pink one. It took courage to step away from the security of the door, and once she did she kept her eyes fixed on the island of light ahead. The black velvet ground was perfectly smooth, without the slightest wrinkle. She could practically skate over it in her flats.

When she reached the floodlamp, she saw it had a pink filter just like the ones Zach used. He got them from the drama department when colored spotlights burned out. And the scene it illuminated was exactly like a print Zach had made—a cardboard silhouette of a neon-pink coyote in the grass. The print had been weird and high tech, like all Zach's photos, but Jenny had always liked it. Just now the coyote-shape standing alone with pink light blazing on it was unnerving.

Waiting for the photographer, Jenny thought. It gave the disquieting impression that it had been waiting there forever.

She headed toward the next floodlamp, a white one maybe forty feet away. It was hard to judge distance here.

This one was shining on a wall, a single wall standing alone, its windows broken out. Silver dots and swathes decorated the wall. Zach had gone into deserted houses in Zuma Beach and painted and photographed them. Vandalism, the police said, but Zach insisted it was art.

Jenny looked on both sides of the freestanding wall. It was unnerving, too. Everything was so quiet here. . . .

Just as she thought it, she heard a faint clanking noise.

The light from the pink floodlamp dimmed for a moment—as if something had passed in front of it. Standing rigid, Jenny strained her eyes in the darkness. She couldn't see anything moving. She couldn't hear anything, either.

Just your imagination, she told herself—but it was hard to make it sound convincing.

Glancing back frequently, she walked to the next lamp.

This one had a neon orange filter. A few years ago Zach had photographed baking soda thrown in the air under colored lights. The problem was that here the baking soda *stayed* in the air, a glowing orange cloud suspended—by nothing. Jenny could see individual motes in it twinkle and drift slightly.

God, get me out of here.

She backed away from it and set out for the next island.

When she got closer her heart skipped and she

began to run. There were two blue floodlamps close together. Zach was under one.

Jenny opened her mouth to shout to him, but stopped at the last minute. What if it *wasn't* Zach? She'd been fooled once.

She approached cautiously and looked down at the figure in silence.

Same flannel shirt over same T-shirt. Same denims. Same hair in same ponytail.

He was holding a fist-size rock over a gray canvas painted with silver streaks. He put the rock down, looked at it, picked it back up. He put it down again in almost exactly the same place.

"I'm going to call it 'Rock on Water,' " he said. He looked up. "Because rocks don't really float."

"Zach," said Jenny. She knelt down and put a hand on his shoulder. His gray eyes were abstracted and a little glazed, just like the other's had been. But something told Jenny this was really her cousin.

A stealthy noise in the endless dark made her look up fast. The white spotlight winked out, went back on.

"Zach, we've got to go," she said and tightened her grip. "I'll explain later—but there's something out there, and we have to get back to the door."

Zach just gave her one of his absent smiles, the kind that didn't reach his eyes. "I know it's out there," he said. "It doesn't matter. It's all part of my hallucination."

"Your *what?* You mean your nightmare?"

"Whatever." He picked up the rock again, shifted it slightly, considered it. "I've known for a long time that this was going to happen."

Jenny was genuinely astonished. "You knew we were going to get kidnapped by the Shadow Man?"

"I knew I was going to go crazy." Then, adjusting the rock fractionally, he said, "Actually 'kidnapped by the Shadow Man' is a really interesting way of putting it. Really imaginative. I mean, what else is going insane?"

Jenny could feel her mouth hanging open. Then she shut it with a snap and took her cousin by both shoulders.

"Zachary, you are not insane," she said. "Is *that* what your problem is—why you were acting so strange before? Because you thought you'd gone *crazy?*"

"Brain kidnapped by the Shadow Man," he told her. "It was bound to happen sooner or later. It runs in the family."

"Oh, for God's sake, Zach!" She had no idea what he was talking about.

The orange floodlamp, the next one out, seemed to flicker.

"Don't worry," Zach told Jenny. "You're just part of my hallucination. It won't really hurt."

"What won't really hurt?"

Zach was gazing at the rock on his canvas. "It's about dimensions. See? The canvas is two dimensional and the—"

An arrow shattered one of the blue floodlamps in a shower of sparks and glass.

No, a bolt, Jenny thought, stunned. A bolt from a crossbow. She recognized it because Zach's father had made it to the National Crossbow Championship three years running. Bolts were even more lethal

165

than arrows—and this one was metal and looked almost futuristic.

Zach was brushing bits of glass off his canvas.

"Zach, *get up!*" Jenny was frantic.

Another bolt shattered the second blue floodlight. Jenny jumped away from the sparks. Zach hunched protectively over his rock.

"Zach, listen to me! This is not a hallucination, it's *real,* and you can die for real here, too! You can bring your rock if you want, but we've got to leave this minute—*this minute!*" Her voice rose hysterically at the end.

It got through to him. She could barely see him by the glow of the white-splattered sky, but he got up—still holding the rock—and went where she was pulling him.

Orange floodlight, Jenny was thinking. Orange, and then white, and then pink. The door should be beyond that.

The orange lamp shattered as they got to it.

"Zach, who's after us? No, don't stop, come on!" Panting, Jenny tugged at his elbow. He'd turned around to look thoughtfully behind them. He didn't seem frightened.

"Me," he said.

They reached the freestanding wall by the white floodlamp. Jenny felt somewhat safer behind it. She looked at her cousin. *"You?"*

"It's me. It's my hallucination and I'm chasing myself. Hunting myself."

"Oh, Zach," she said helplessly. Then: "Zach, it's not a hallucination. The same thing is happening to all of us—we're all here. Dee and Mike and Tom and

Audrey and me. And Summer was here, but her nightmare *killed* her because she couldn't cope. So you have to cope, because if you don't . . ." Jenny's eyes were wet.

Zach blinked. "We're all here? It's real?"

"It's real. It really happened, the Game and the Shadow Man and everything. It's not in your head. It almost drove me crazy, too, but you can't let it."

Zach blinked again, then looked through the empty window of the wall, out into the darkness. "If it's real . . ." he began slowly, and continued in a voice with more strength, "If it's real, then who's that?"

Jenny inched over to take a cautious peek. A—person—was standing at the very edge of the light that went through the window. His crossbow *was* futuristic-looking—and so was he. Cyberpunk, Jenny thought. He was wearing black body armor that hugged his lean body sleekly, and he had one normal hand and one that was shining steel and cables. There was some kind of high-tech gun strapped to his thigh.

He wore a helmet with a mirrored face mask that completely obscured his features.

Jenny leaned back against the wall.

"Oh, terrific," she whispered.

"I figured he was my dark side. The part of me that wants to destroy me," Zach said reasonably.

A bolt came through the window—Jenny felt the wind of it—and shattered the white floodlamp.

"Come on!"

This time Zach ran without prompting.

The Cyber-Hunter got to the pink floodlight before them.

He couldn't have, but he did anyway. He stood, backlit by the neon pink glow, a dark silhouette as they approached.

"This way! We have to get to the door!"

Jenny veered sharply, circling to get to the other side of the pink lamp. Zach followed her. But when she got to the place where the door should have been, it wasn't.

"It's *gone!*" Jenny turned to look back. The Cyber-Hunter was facing them now, facing the blazing pink glow.

And what on earth are we supposed to do with him? Jenny thought. Kill him? Bash him with the rock? I don't think so.

One thing she'd learned—the nightmares were fair. There was always a chance, a way to get out, even when there didn't seem to be. She supposed Julian considered that only sporting.

So what could they do with the Cyber-Hunter? How could Zach face his fear?

"Zach," she said hesitantly, "you haven't seen his face, right? You don't know if he *looks* like you."

"No, I just figured. He's like the high-tech stuff in my photos—come to get me."

And like some cyberpunk stuff I've seen, Jenny thought grimly. She said, "If you *did* look at him . . . If you pulled off his helmet, say—"

She could feel Zach recoil in the dark.

Jenny shut her eyes, feeling suddenly tired. "Then that's what you have to do, I think. It's your night-mare, and you have to face him. I'll go with you."

It was a risk. Whether the Hunter was Julian or just one of Julian's dream-creatures, like the dark elves or the small Visitors, he might very well look like Zach under the helmet.

"Zach, I think you have to—or we won't ever find the way out of here. I think, even if he looks like you, you have to know he's *not* you."

"But—if he is me . . . if you're not really here and this is all my hallucination . . ."

"Then I'll probably disappear or something!" Jenny said. "And then at least you'll *know* you're crazy. All I know is that Summer wouldn't face her nightmare and she *died.*"

There was a silence. Zach turned toward her, but it was too dark to be sure of his expression. "Come on," he said and started for the light.

Jenny's heart rate kept accelerating as they got closer to it. The Cyber-Hunter could easily shoot them at any minute.

He didn't. He stood as still as a figure in the Movieland Wax Museum. He was exactly Zach's height.

Zach stopped when they were a few feet in front of him.

Jenny could hear blood roaring in her ears.

The Cyber-Hunter shifted the crossbow a little. Pink jewels of light slid up and down it, and over his black armor. Zach's face was reflected in the mirrored faceplate.

"Go on, Zach," Jenny whispered. "Take off the helmet. Tell him he's not you, whatever he looks like."

She wasn't nearly as confident as she sounded. Was it Zach's face under the helmet? Julian's? Maybe it was some hideous android—some kind of killer robot. Maybe Zach would get shot before he could find out. Maybe . . .

The Cyber-Hunter stood waiting.

With a sudden gesture Zach reached out and grabbed the front of the helmet, pulling the face mask away.

There was nothing underneath.

No face, no head. Jenny, prepared for anything else, screamed involuntarily. The Cyber-Hunter's black body armor fell down empty, the crossbow clattering on top of it.

A door appeared beside the pink floodlight.

Zach was staring down at the empty shell of armor. He nudged the dismembered robotic hand with his foot.

Jenny gave a little gasp of relief. It had been so easy—but then she looked at her cousin. The real test was in his head. "I'm still here, Zach," she said. "Right? Right?"

He turned to look at her, pink light haloing his hair.

Then, slowly, he smiled. "Right," he said.

The awful dazed look had disappeared. He looked like Zach again. She could *see* the sanity return to his eyes. Relief flooded Jenny in painful waves.

Zach dropped the mirrored face mask on the pile of black armor.

"The rock I'll keep. I still want to do that photo."

They stepped through the door to the mirrored hallway.

Zach's slip of paper was on the ground. Jenny picked it up and frowned over it. She could vaguely make out what looked like a profile—a profile with a

170

beaky nose—but behind that was just a futuristic mishmash of colors, streaks and dabs.

"The things in my head," Zach said. He took it from her and tore it up. Jenny watched the colored pieces float down like confetti.

"Zach—what made you think insanity runs in the family?"

Zach just shrugged. The others had explained their nightmares, but it didn't surprise Jenny that Zach wouldn't. Zach protected his privacy.

An unseen clock struck four.

"I hate this place," Zach said, looking at his own gray-eyed reflection. "It reminds me of the fun house at that amusement park we used to go to when we were kids."

"Then *you're* the one who put it here," Jenny said. She'd forgotten the fun house herself—but then she'd forgotten a lot about her childhood, especially the years before she came to California. She didn't want to remember.

She felt a little twist of premonition in her stomach.

She also felt the heat in her cheeks. Now that they were out of danger, now that Zach looked like himself again, she found that her attitude toward him had changed. It was Julian's fault. Jenny knew perfectly well that her cousin had never thought of her romantically—but she couldn't forget what had happened in the darkroom. Every time she looked at Zach, she remembered seeing those gray eyes black with passion.

I'll forget eventually, she told herself. It'll wear off. Just as long as he never finds out.

Aloud she said, "We've got to find the others. Dee and Audrey and Mike are all wandering around here somewhere. I guess"—she hesitated—"I guess we should separate. But I'm afraid we might not be able to find our way back to each other. I know it seems as if the hall only goes two ways, but you can't trust anything here."

"Wait a minute." Zach pulled two crayons out of the pocket of his flannel shirt. "I took them because I thought the colors might work in a photo. Take your pick, cadet blue or Indian red. We can mark a trail."

Jenny chose cadet blue and made a pale, waxy streak on the nearest mirror. "Brilliant," she said. "I'll go this way, you go that way. Whoever finds them can bring them back here."

"Where the two crayons meet," Zach said and began a line of his own. Still drawing, he walked away. The first zigzag of the hall took him out of sight.

No thank-you, no goodbye. Well, *that* should help her forget the darkroom scene. Zach was himself again, all right.

She went her own way, leaving a crayon trail behind her.

The mirrored hallway seemed infinite—and completely deserted. It went on and on with no variations.

Until, to her astonishment, she came to the end.

It was a blank wall, gray as concrete. No mirror, no blue light, no red button.

It scared her.

On the ground in front of it was a white slip of paper.

172

Jenny approached the paper slowly. It scared her, too. Dee, Audrey, Mike, Summer, and Zach had had their nightmares. And Julian had said Tom was at the top of the house.

Nobody's nightmare left on this floor but hers.

She picked the paper up, turned it over. She recognized the formless doodle around the edges. The middle of the paper was exactly as she'd left it—blank.

Jenny looked up at the blank wall.

"Need any help?" Julian asked from behind her.

The paper crumpled in Jenny's clenched fist as she turned.

He was leaning against a mirror, wearing the sleek black body armor. No helmet, though. Instead, there was a splash of purple in the shock of white hair falling over his forehead and a triangular blue design on his cheekbone. It looked almost like silk-screening. More cyberpunk, Jenny thought. High-tech body art. Zach would love it—or maybe not.

Jenny looked straight into the strange cat-tilted blue eyes. Things had changed since Julian had set the bees on her. She had a new confidence at her core. Whatever he did to her, even if he killed her, he couldn't break her.

"So it was you shooting at us," she said.

"Personally, I think it was Zach's father. I think he has a little complex there. Rugged, old-fashioned dad; artistic, newfangled son, you know. On the other hand, I *am* a hunter." He pushed the lock of purple hair out of his eyes, smiling.

"Why don't you just go away?" Jenny said. "I'm trying to figure something out."

"I'm glad to help. I know a lot about you. I've watched you for so many years now. Hour after hour, day after day."

Jenny froze. He'd said similar things before, and she hadn't really listened. Or she hadn't taken it literally. But now, looking at him, she knew he meant it.

It was the most terrible thing she'd ever heard.

He'd *watched* her for hours on end? How many times in her life, when she'd thought she was alone, had he been there?

It was an appalling intimacy, and one Jenny didn't want.

"I'm in love with you," he said simply. "I think everything you do is marvelous."

"You—"

"There's no need to be embarrassed. I don't think the same way you do. Whether your hair's brushed —whether your makeup is on—I don't care. Besides"—he smiled at her—"didn't you know that I was there?"

"Of course not." But she had, Jenny realized. Somewhere deep inside herself she'd known she was being watched. She'd just thought everybody had that feeling.

Those times in the night when she woke up, certain that a tall shape was standing over her in the darkness. Usually when it happened she couldn't move, could hardly breathe. Sometimes she would actually *see* the shape, the outline black against lighter blackness, and she stared until her eyes ached.

If she kicked at it or turned on the light, it would disappear. But she'd sit there breathing hard anyway, choking on her own fear.

Her room always looked strange in that unnatural middle-of-the-night brightness. Subtly different than it did in the daytime. It was always a long time before she would be able to turn the light off again.

And underneath, in her heart of hearts, she would feel it had been real. Not just a dream. Her eyes had been open when she'd seen the thing above her, and it didn't matter if that was stupid and nobody could see in such darkness. She'd seen it anyway. It had been there.

Jenny had thought everybody went through things like that.

"I hate you," she whispered.

"I'd have thought you'd want my help right now." He nodded at the blank wall. *"That's* your nightmare, Jenny—but how are you going to get into it? And if you can't get into it, how are you going to get through it?"

He wants you panicked, Jenny told herself. He wants to scare you, to make you think you need his help.

But she didn't need it. She *refused* to need it.

She smiled suddenly. She could feel it was lopsided. She held up the cadet blue crayon.

"I'll get in with this," she said and smoothed out her blank slip of paper.

His eyelids drooped in amusement, and his voice was a caress. "But how will you *remember?* You don't know what to draw. You've spent all these years trying to forget. . . ."

"I know enough," Jenny said. She wondered just how much Julian knew about her own private nightmare, the one she'd spent so long running away from.

She had the chilling feeling that she was about to find out.

"I know what it starts with," she said. "It starts with my grandfather's basement, when I was five years old."

She put the paper flat against a mirror and began to draw.

13

Cadet blue, which had just looked pale on the mirror, turned out to be gray on paper.

Jenny was no artist, but she could draw simple things. Like a square—that was her grandfather's basement. Steps, going out of the top of the picture up to the house. A desk against one wall. A couch. Three or four large bookcases.

That was all she could remember. She hoped it was enough.

Glancing over her shoulder, she saw that Julian was gone again. Good.

She put the slip of paper on the floor in front of the blank wall.

The flash of light was exactly like a flashgun going off in her eyes, leaving her with dancing afterimages. Score one for Zach, she thought. When she could see again, she found herself looking in a mirror.

It had worked.

She could feel her pulse in her wrists and throat as well as her chest. God, don't let me run away, she thought.

After so many years of fighting *not* to remember this, she was going to throw herself right into it. It was going to be bad. How bad, she'd have to find out when it happened.

She pressed the red button. The blue light went on. The mirrored door slid open.

She didn't give herself a chance to look at anything before she stepped inside.

Golden sunlight slanted in from small windows set high on the walls. To Jenny's utter surprise she felt a thrill of excitement and recognition.

I remember those windows! I remember . . .

The door slid shut behind her, but she was already stepping out to the center of the room, looking around in wonder. Taking in the colors, the profusion of objects.

It's smaller than I thought it would be—and even more crowded. But it's my grandfather's basement.

Her grandfather, though, wasn't there.

That's right. He wasn't here that day. I remember. I let myself in the house and went looking for him, but I couldn't find him anywhere upstairs.

So . . . I looked down here—I think. I must have. I don't remember doing it, but I must have.

Jenny turned toward the stairs, which ended in a blank wall at the top. No door, of course, because this was a nightmare. The wall was as blank as her mind—her sense of delighted recognition had stopped cold. She had no idea what came next.

But as she stared, she seemed to see the ghost of a child looking down from the top step. A little girl wearing shorts, with wind-ruffled hair and a scab on her knee.

Herself. At age five.

It was almost like watching a movie. She could see the little girl's thongs flap as she ran down the stairs. She could see the child's lips open as she called for her grandfather, see the child standing in surprise at the bottom when he turned out not to be down here.

As long as Jenny watched without trying to guide the images, the ghostly movie went on.

The little girl was looking around, green eyes opening wide as she realized that she was *alone* down here, a thing which had never happened before.

That's right. The door to the basement had always been locked when Jenny's grandfather wasn't down there—but not that day. Jenny remembered the feeling of delicious wickedness at being where she wasn't allowed to be. But she couldn't remember what happened next.

Don't try to remember. You're trying too hard. Relax and *see* what happens.

As soon as she did, she seemed to see the little girl again. The ghostly image was standing uncertainly, swaying on her toes, considering whether to stay or go.

It was stay. The child looked around with elaborate casualness, then, sucking on her lower lip and affecting an air of nonchalance, she wandered over to the first bookcase.

All right, Jenny thought. So let's see what's in the bookcase. She followed the child's image. The little girl was idly running a grimy finger along a row of books—which, of course, she couldn't read. Not even the titles. But sixteen-year-old Jenny could.

Some of them looked fairly normal, like Goethe's *Faust* and *UFO's: A New Look*. But others were completely unfamiliar, like *The Qabalah* and *De Occulta Philosophia* and *The Galdrabók*.

The little girl was moving on to the second book-case, which held all sorts of objects. One whole shelf was crowded with small wooden boxes with glass tops, filled with what looked like spices. No—herbs, Jenny thought. Dried herbs.

The little girl was running fascinated fingers over some balls of colored glass attached to strings. Sixteen-year-old Jenny was more interested in the looped cross next to them—she was sure it was an ankh. Summer's dad had said the ankh was an Egyptian life symbol that kept away bad luck.

And that diamond-shaped thing made of yarn— that was a Mexican Eye of God. A string design that was supposed to protect you from evil. Jenny's mother had one in the kitchen, for decoration.

But what about the bracelet of cobalt and tur-quoise beads, alternating with little silver charms? And the gold-plated religious pictures? And the wooden flute wrapped in fur?

. . . items of protection? Jenny thought. She wasn't sure what put the idea in her mind, but the longer she looked at the things in this bookcase, the more certain she felt.

But . . . it wasn't just this bookcase. Slowly Jenny turned to look around the basement again. All these things, all these beautiful, exotic things—could they *all* be for protection?

Who would need that much protection? And why?

The little girl was fingering a large silver bell in the bookcase, but Jenny's eyes were drawn to a group of charts on the wall. *The Theban Alphabet,* one was labeled, and underneath were strange symbols. *The Alphabet of the Magi. The Secret Etruscan Alphabet. The Celtic Tree Alphabet. Numerical Values of the Hebrew Alphabet.* There was also a rather frightening engraving of a skeleton holding a raven on one bony hand.

The ghost child was moving again, wandering over to the large writing desk. Going on tiptoe in her thongs, she leaned her elbows on the felt desk pad. Jenny found herself looking down through a transparent blond head at the papers there.

Lots of papers—which held no interest for the five-year-old Jenny except that she wasn't supposed to touch them. Intrinsic naughtiness was the fun.

Sixteen-year-old Jenny could read them. One was a chart like those on the wall. It was titled *The Elder Futhark* but Jenny recognized the slanty, angular symbols.

Runes.

Like the ones she'd seen on the drinking horns of the young men in the forest. Like the one on the inside cover of the white box. Each had its name written beside it in her grandfather's strong black handwriting, with notes.

Uruz, she read. For piercing the veil between the worlds. She recognized the inverted *U* shape, the two uneven horns pointing downward.

Raidho—it was shaped like an *R* drawn without any curved lines—for journeying in space or time.

Dagaz, which looked like an hourglass on its side. For awakening.

One of the runes was circled with a thick pen stroke.

Nauthiz, Jenny read. Shaped like a backward-leaning *X,* with one stroke longer than the other. For containment.

The last word was underlined heavily.

Jenny took another slow look around the room.

Oh, my God.

She couldn't keep the truth away any longer. She'd been holding it at arm's length, refusing to look at it, but now it burst on her with the force of absolute certainty. There was no way to deny it.

Oh, my God, he was a *sorcerer.*

Her mother's father had been a sorcerer.

Don't think about it . . . don't remember, the voice in her mind whispered. Nobody can *make* you remember. Stay safe behind your walls, or else . . .

It was going to be very bad from here on, she realized.

She had to remember—for Tom. But Tom's image eluded her. So much had happened since she'd seen him last night—could it only be last night? She'd changed so much since then. She tried to conjure up his rakish smile in her mind, his green-flecked eyes, but the picture she got was like a distant, faded photograph. Somebody she'd known long ago.

God, I can't get any *feeling* for him.

Her palms were tingling. Her stomach felt sick.

I still have to remember. For Dee. For Zach. For Audrey and Michael—and Summer. *Yes.* For Summer.

All the others had faced their nightmares. Even Summer had tried. Pictures skittered through Jenny's mind: Dee thrashing like an animal; Audrey huddled and moaning; Michael screaming; Summer's blue-white lips; Zach's glazed gray eyes. They'd all been terrified out of their wits. Was Jenny's nightmare any worse than theirs?

Yes, I think so, the little voice in her mind whispered, but Jenny wasn't listening anymore. From *Don't remember, don't remember,* the chant in her head had changed to *Remember, remember . . .*

Maybe this will help, she told herself rather calmly, and with a feeling of meeting her doom she picked up a leather-bound book on the desk.

It was a journal of sorts. Or at least a record of some kind of experiment. Her grandfather's heavy black writing degenerated into a scrawl in places, but certain sentences stood out clearly as she leafed through.

". . . out of all the methods from different cultures this one seems safest . . . the rune Nyd or Nauthiz provides an eternal constraint, preventing travel in any direction. . . . The rune must be carved, then stained with blood, and finally charged with power by pronouncing its name aloud. . . ."

Jenny flipped through more pages to a later entry.

". . . interesting treatise on the traditional methods of dealing with a *djinn,* or, as the Hausa call them, the *aljunnu.* Why anyone should think this could be accomplished with a bottle is beyond me. . . . I believe the space I've prepared to be just barely sufficient for containing the tremendous energies involved. . . ."

Good grief, he sounded just like a scientist. A mad scientist, Jenny thought. She flipped more pages.

". . . I have achieved the containment at last! I'm very satisfied . . . foolproof methods . . . not the slightest danger . . . the tremendous forces I've harnessed . . . all in complete safety. . . ."

Toward the end there was something stuck in between the pages like a bookmark. It was a torn sheet of yellowing, brittle paper. It looked very old. The writing on it was quite different from her grandfather's—thin and shaky—and part of it was obscured by rusty-brown stains.

It was a poem. There was no title, but the author's name, Johannes Eckhart, and the date, 1943, were scrawled at the top.

I, slipping on the slime-edged stones,
To that dark place by rusty foxfire lit,
Where they lie watching, fingering old bones,
Go with my question. Deep into the pit
Of the Black Forest, where the Erlking rules
And truth is told but always at a cost,
I take my puzzle. Like the other fools
Who've slipped on these same stones and played
      and lost
I come because I must. I have no choice.
The Game is timeless and . . .

The rest of it was covered with the dark stains, except for the last two lines:

I leave them waiting there below.
I hear them laughing as I go.

Jenny leaned back and let out her breath.

Obviously this poem had impressed her grandfather enough for him to keep it for forty years. She knew her grandfather had fought in World War II—he'd been a prisoner in a German POW camp. Maybe he'd met this Johannes Eckhart then. And maybe this Johannes Eckhart had started him thinking. . . .

She had all the pieces of the puzzle now. She just didn't want to put them together. All she could think about was taking the next step in the drama she was playing out here.

The final step, she thought.

The ghostly child in the thongs had vanished; the internal movie had stopped running. But Jenny didn't try to get it back. She could feel the irresistible tug of real memory at last, and she knew what she had to do.

She stepped back to look at the third bookcase.

It was a massive one built of solid mahogany, and it usually stood against the same wall as the desk. Today it had been moved. Pulled out at an angle. The dust pattern on the wall behind it showed clearly where it normally rested.

It had been moved to expose a door behind it.

Jenny hadn't noticed the door before because the case stuck out enough to block it. You had to actually walk beyond the bookcase to get a good look.

That's what Jenny felt compelled to do now.

It was a perfectly ordinary-looking door. Probably leading to a closet. The only strange thing about it was the huge backward-leaning *X* deeply carved into the wood.

Carved and colored a rusty brown like the stains on the poem.

The internal movie had started up again, even

though Jenny didn't need or want it. The ghostly little girl was standing in surprise in front of the door, swaying from one foot to the other. Obviously temptation was fighting with obedience—and winning. The wind-ruffled hair was shaken back, the tanned legs flashed, two small hands grasped the doorknob—and the ghost disappeared.

And then I opened it, Jenny thought. But no image of opening it, or of what had happened after, would come to her mind. She was going to have to find that out for herself.

All the way to the door her heart was thudding wild disapproval. Her body seemed to have more sense than she did. No-don't-no-don't, no-don't-no-don't, her racing pulse said.

Jenny took hold of the knob. The thudding became a screaming.

No, *don't*. Don't—don't—*don't*. . . .

She flung open the door.

Ice and shadows.

That was all she could see. The closet was wide and very deep, and the inside of it was a whirling, seething mixture of white and black. Frost coated the walls, icicles hung like teeth from the ceiling. A blast of freezing wind went straight through Jenny, chilling her as if she'd been plunged into Arctic waters. The tips of her fingers went numb, the skin shriveling.

It was so cold it stopped her breath. It stopped her from moving. The ice was so bright it blinded her.

She got just one glimpse of what was at the center of that whirlpool of light and dark.

Eyes.

Dark eyes, watching eyes, sardonic, cruel, amused eyes. Ancient eyes. Jenny recognized them. They were the eyes she sometimes saw just at the moment of falling asleep or of waking up. The eyes she saw at night in her room.

Eyes in the shadows. Evil, malicious, knowing eyes.

One pair was an indescribably beautiful blue.

She didn't have the air to scream; her lungs were rebelling against the freezing wind she was trying to draw into them. But she had to scream—she had to do something—because they were coming out. *The eyes were coming out.*

It was as if they were coming from very far away, rushing toward her, riding the storm. She had to move—she had to run. The glittery black eyes of the alien Visitors, the slanted eyes of the dark elves—Jenny had thought those were frightening, but they were nothing compared to this. They were feeble, petty imitations. No horror that human beings had invented to scare themselves came anywhere close. Vampires, aliens, werewolves, ghouls, they were all *nothing*. Stories made up to hide the real fear.

The terror that came in the darkness, the one that *everyone* knew about, and everyone forgot. Only sometimes, waking up between dreams, did the full realization hit. And even then it was seldom remembered, and if it was remembered it was dismissed the next morning. The knowledge couldn't survive in daylight. But at night sometimes people glimpsed the truth. That humans weren't alone.

They shared the world with *them*.

The Others.

The Watchers.

The Hunters.

The Shadow Men.

The ones who walked freely through the human world, and who had another world of their own. They'd been called different things in different ages, but their true nature always came through.

They granted favors—sometimes. They always asked for something in return, usually more than you could afford.

They liked games, riddles, any kind of play. But they were unreliable—whimsical. They balanced any good they did with capricious evil.

They preyed on humans. When people lost time, *they* were responsible. When people disappeared, *they* were laughing. People who got into *their* world usually didn't get back.

They had power. Trying to get a good look at them—or trap them—was always a bad idea. Even being too curious about them could kill you.

One more thing. They were heartbreakingly beautiful.

All this passed through Jenny's mind in a matter of seconds. She didn't need to reason it out. She *knew.* It was as if a crust had fallen away from her mind, and she saw the truth as a complete, coherent whole. All she could think was, *So that's it. I remember now.*

The eyes were still rushing toward her. Her loose hair whipped around her face in the wind, her own breath coating it with ice. She couldn't move.

"Jenny!"

Her name called in a terrible voice. Before she

could turn, she was caught around the waist and lifted—lifted as if she were five years old and weighed thirty-seven pounds.

"Grandpa," she gasped and threw her arms around his neck.

He was smaller than she remembered, too—and just now his tired, kind face was etched in absolute horror. Jenny tried to cling to him, but he slung her around, thrusting her behind the bookcase.

"Nauthiz! Nauthiz!" he shouted.

He was trying to shut the door, tracing over the rune on the front with stabs of his finger. His slashing motions as he traced the *X* became more and more violent, and his voice was the most dreadful thing Jenny had ever heard. *"Nauthiz!"*

The door wouldn't shut. The old man's shouts were becoming screams of despair.

A white light was coming from the closet. A white storm, with tendrils and lashings of mist. Dark strands were interwoven with the white. The tendrils were writhing around Jenny's grandfather.

Jenny tried to scream. She couldn't.

The wind blasted out, blowing her grandfather's sparse hair. All his clothes were rippling. Frost flowed out on the ceiling, down to the desk, to the ground-level windows. It spread like crystals growing along the walls.

Tears froze in Jenny's eyes. She seemed to be locked in the form of a stricken five-year-old. She couldn't make herself go to him.

The voices that spoke from the mist were as cold as the wind. Like bells made of ice.

"We won't be put back. . . ."

"You know the laws. . . ."

"We have a claim, now. . . ."

And her grandfather's voice, full of desperate fear. "Anything else. You can have anything else—"

"She broke the rune. . . ."

". . . set us free . . ."

". . . and we want her."

"Give her to us." This was all the voices together.

"I can't!" her grandfather said. It was almost a groan.

"Then we'll *take* her. . . ."

"We'll embrace her. . . ."

"No, let's keep her," said a voice full of subtle, elemental music. Like water running over rock. "I want her."

"We all want her. . . ."

". . . We're all *hungry.*"

"No," said Jenny's grandfather.

A voice like an ice floe cracking said, "There's only one way to change the consequences. Make a new bargain."

Jenny's grandfather's jaw worked, and he backed away from the closet a few steps. "You mean . . ."

"A life for a life."

"Someone must take her place."

"Come now, that's only fair."

The voices were delicate, reasonable. Evil. Only the water-voice seemed to have an objection.

"I *want* her. . . ." it argued.

"Ah, youth," said a voice as slow as a glacier, and all of them laughed like Christmas bells.

"I'm ready," said Jenny's grandfather.

"No!" Jenny screamed.

She could move at last—but it was too late. She remembered everything now. She had been cowering behind the bookcase, her five-year-old mind probably better able to deal with the reality of the Shadow Men than an adult's. They were the monsters that scare every five-year-old. The Bogeymen. The Bad Things. And they were taking her grandfather.

She'd jumped up then and run, as she was running now. Toward the closet. Toward the white tendrils of mist that were coiling around her grandfather, toward the ice storm of eyes. She'd heard her grandfather screaming that day as the storm dragged him into the closet. She'd reached for him, catching his flailing hand. She'd been screaming, too, just as she was screaming now, and the freezing wind had been howling around her, full of angry, evil, *ravenous* voices.

For one instant, then as now, it had been a horrible tug-of-war. She, Jenny, clinging on to her grandfather's hand with all her strength. *They,* in the ice storm, pulling him away. Into the depths of a closet that had become endless, a tunnel reaching to some other world.

She could never hope to stop them, of course. She succeeded only in being dragged along the floor, her clothes torn, her shoes lost, her bare feet raking up ice.

They were both going in.

Then her grandfather slapped her hands away.

Hitting and scratching, he tore out of her grip. Jenny fell on the floor, the ice cold under her bare legs. She was directly in front of the closet, and she had a perfect view of the screaming, whirling pinwheel that had been a man, disappearing into a white cloud which got smaller and smaller as if speeding away and finally disappeared itself, becoming a closet wall.

Then the shrieking wind stopped and the room was empty and Jenny was sobbing alone in the silence.

14

*J*enny?" Dee's voice said hesitantly. "Jenny, are you okay?"

I've had such a strange dream, Jenny thought, but when she lifted her face from her hands, it was real. She was sitting on the floor of her grandfather's basement, in a puddle of icy-cold water. Dee, Audrey, Zach, and Michael were standing in another puddle, looking at her.

"I found these three in the hallway," Zach said.

"We fell down a shaft," Michael said. "This hole just opened up in front of us. It took us all the way back to the first floor."

"It was a chute," said Dee. "I fell down it, too, and then we had to walk back up here."

"We followed your crayon trail, and it ended at a door," Zach finished. "We pressed the button and . . ."

"It let us in," Audrey said crisply, when he

stopped. "But it looks like something's already happened."

"My nightmare," Jenny said. She was having a very hard time bringing herself back to the present. The five-year-old in her mind seemed more real than the sixteen-year-old these people were talking to. Dee and Michael and Audrey looked like strangers.

Not Zach, because Zach had been there when she was five.

Zach, maybe, understood this. In any case he knelt on the floor beside her, ignoring the water soaking into his jeans.

"What happened?" he said, his gray eyes steady.

"I lost," Jenny said dully, feeling strangely removed from everything. "I screwed up. I couldn't save him. I lost."

"It's something about Grandpa Evenson, isn't it?"

"What do you know about it?"

Zach hesitated, then, looking her directly in the face, he said, "Only what my parents told me. They say he—went crazy that day. Tried to—well, hurt you."

Jenny was shocked out of her apathy. *"What?"*

"They found you here, in the basement, with your clothes all torn and your arms all scratched. Your legs and feet were bleeding. . . ."

"From the ice," Jenny whispered. "I got dragged through the ice. And he scratched my hands to make me let him go. They were taking him. He let them take him instead of me."

Then, suddenly, she was sobbing again. She felt a movement, then a slender, hard arm around her. Dee. A rustle and a cool hand on her wrist. Audrey, heedless of her fancy clothes. An awkward, warm grip from behind on her shoulder. Michael. They were all around her, all trying to help.

"You went through our nightmares with all of us," Audrey said softly. "It's not fair you had to face yours alone."

Jenny shook her head. "You don't understand. All of you had nightmares about things you were scared *might* happen. Mine *did* happen—because of me. It was real. It was my fault."

"Tell us," Dee said, her face stern and beautiful.

"He was a sorcerer," Jenny said. She looked at Zach. "You mean, all this time everybody thought he tried to hurt me?"

"What were they supposed to think?" Zach said. "You were here, practically in a coma. You screamed if anyone tried to touch you, but you wouldn't talk. And he was gone. They figured he ran away when he realized what he tried to do. And when they looked around at this place"—Zach looked around the basement himself and snorted—"well, they knew he was crazy. Paranoid. Because all this junk turned out to be—"

"Charms for protection," Jenny said.

"Right. I mean, what kind of nut collects thousands of those from all over the world? And he had piles of books on the occult, all kinds of garbage. . . ."

"He was a sorcerer," Jenny said again. "Not a black one. Maybe not a white one, either, but not black. He wasn't trying to do evil. He was just—a little bit naive. He didn't allow for accidents happening . . . like a five-year-old coming down here on a day he didn't expect her, and opening a door she knew she shouldn't touch."

"That door?" Dee looked at the empty closet.

Jenny nodded.

"But what was in the closet? A monster?"

"Julian."

They all stared at her.

Jenny swallowed the bad taste in her mouth. "My grandfather wanted—well, the same thing those German boys in the forest wanted, I guess." She looked at Audrey. "Power. Or maybe he was just curious. He knew there were—things—out in the darkness, and he caught some. Maybe he used runes to summon them up, I don't know. But I know he used a rune to hold them. On that door."

"And just what," Michael said, his voice unusually grim, "would you call the things he caught?"

"Aliens," Jenny said, looking at Dee. "Dark elves," she said, looking at Audrey. "Demons," she said, turning around to face Michael. "The Shadow Men," she said to Zach.

Dee hissed softly in comprehension.

Once started, Jenny couldn't seem to stop. "Dakaki. The Erlking. The old gods. The fairy folk . . ."

"Okay," Michael said huskily. "Enough, already."

"They're *real,*" Jenny said. "They've *always* been here—like genies, you know? The old name for a genie was *djinn,* and in his notes my grandfather called them *aljunnu.* Djinn—aljunnu—Julian—get it? It was a joke. They like to *play* with us. . . ."

Her voice was rising. She felt herself gripped from all sides, but she went on.

"He was keeping them trapped—but *I* let them out, and that changed everything. They said they had

196

the right to take me. But he went instead. He did it for me." She stopped.

"If we're going to get through this," Dee said, "we've got to be strong. We've got to stand together. All right?"

"Right," Audrey said, the first to confirm it. Looking down, Jenny saw Audrey's perfectly polished nails entwined with Dee's slender dark fingers. Both holding on to each other, to Jenny.

"Right," Zach said with no hesitation, no distance in his winter-gray eyes. His long-fingered artist's hand came down over Dee's and Audrey's.

"Right," whispered Michael, and he gripped Zach's hand with his own square pudgy fingers, unembarrassed.

"But there's nothing to *do*," Jenny said, almost crying again. "He won. I lost. I didn't make it through my nightmare. That door"—nodding at the closet one—"was always here. It's not the way out."

"What about that one?" Michael said, standing back and looking up the stairs.

Jenny had to move around the bookcase to see it. Instead of the blank wall she had seen earlier at the top of the staircase, there was a door.

Directly above them—in the room above—a clock struck five.

"You must have done something right," Dee said.

Jenny's skirt was clammy, clinging to her legs. Her hair, she knew, was in complete disarray. She was exhausted and still shaking inside, and it seemed like years since she had slept.

"I'll go first," she said and led them up the stairs, trying to look like Dee, proud as a princess. She found her slip of paper on the top step and stepped on it.

"If that's the turret—the top of the house—we've won," Audrey said. "Right?"

Somehow Jenny didn't think it was going to be that easy.

She twisted the knob and pushed, and the door swung back on oiled hinges. They all stepped into the room above. It was much larger than any turret could possibly be.

It was the More Games store.

Well, more or less, Jenny thought. There were the same shelves and racks and tables with the same uncanny games on them. There was the same small window—quite dark—and the same lamps with shades of purple and red and blue glass.

But there were differences, too. One was the grandfather clock standing near a corner, ticking loudly and steadily.

The other was Tom.

Jenny ran to him. He was huddled against the clock, chained to it somehow. Her mind registered fury at the humiliation of that, then went on to more important things.

"Tommy," she said, reaching with both hands for him.

He turned weakly, and Jenny was shocked. There were no bruises on his face, but he looked—ravaged. His skin was unhealthily pale, and there were black circles under his eyes. He gave her the ghost of his own rakish smile.

"Hey, Thorny," he said painfully.

Jenny put her face against his shoulder and cried.

The faded-photograph memory had disappeared.

What Jenny remembered now was the day of their first kiss, in second grade, behind the hibiscus bushes at George Washington Elementary School. They'd both gotten detention, but it had been worth it.

That kiss, she thought. Everything innocent. Everything sweet. Tom hadn't been arrogant, then, hadn't taken anything for granted. Tom had loved her.

"Tommy," she said. "I missed you so much. What did he do to you?"

Tom shook his head. "Hardly anything . . . I don't understand. There were the rats"—his haunted eyes skittered around the floor—"but they're gone now."

Rats. So that was what Tom had seen in the parlor—the invisible things that had tried to climb up his legs. In second grade Tom had owned a turtle, and his older brother Greg had owned a pet rat. One morning they woke up to find that the rat had eaten the turtle—eaten it right out of the shell.

I knew how upset that made him—how much he hated rats after that, Jenny thought. Why didn't I realize what they were in the parlor?

Because it hadn't seemed bad enough. Tom had been *so* afraid. But one thing Jenny had learned: Everybody's nightmare was scariest to them. You had to see it with them, get into their shoes, to understand just how scary.

"I'm sorry," she whispered. "But, oh, Tom, your wrists—" They were torn, bleeding. He was wearing shackles like the kind his brother Bruce used in police work. The rest of him was wrapped up like Marley's ghost.

"I kept trying to get away," he said. "Not because of the rats. Because I saw you. He would come and

199

hold up a mirror, and I could see you and what was happening to you. I saw you go through everything. When Summer died . . ." He stopped to get control of himself, his face twisting.

Saw me? Jenny thought in horror. Pictures of what Tom might have seen when she and Julian were together flashed through her mind. Then she felt a backwash of relief. If Julian had been standing here holding a mirror, he must have been showing Tom the times when he—Julian—wasn't with Jenny. Still, she had to know.

"Did you ever see—him—in the mirror?"

"No. But he told me—he told me he was doing things to you. To all of you. He laughed about it."

Jenny gripped both his hands. "Don't you worry about him, Tom. He can't hurt us anymore. We're free, Tom—we've *won.* Now we just need to find the way out of here."

Tom looked at her, then nodded behind her. Jenny turned.

She'd missed it before, because Tom had so quickly captured her attention. There was a door, just like the door in the More Games store that led out onto Montevideo Street. But this door was partly open, showing darkness outside.

Standing before it, completely blocking the way, were a giant coiled snake and a large wolf.

"The Creeper and the Lurker. At last," Dee said.

"Just a slight problem," Michael said nervously.

They weren't real animals exactly—they looked more as if they'd been painted with luminous paint on the darkness. Like some special effect Zach might make for a photo. But the wolf breathed and the snake's fluorescent tongue flicked in and out. Jenny felt sure that they could move—and do harm.

She fingered Tom's chains. "He has to let us go. The rules were that if we got to the top of the house, we could go free."

"Not exactly," the liquid, elemental voice said from the back of the store.

He was dressed the way he had been in the More Games store, in that weird combination of cyberpunk and Byronic poet. The snake tattoo was back on his wrist.

He looked as laconic as he had in the store, and as beautiful. His hair was like moonstone, white with a shimmery blue glow inside. In this dim light his eyes were midnight blue.

He looked—charming, sinister, and slightly mad. A demon prince with the face of an angel.

Jenny was suddenly very frightened.

And much more alert. Seeing Julian cleared the cobwebs out of your brain instantly. She straightened her back, still kneeling.

The others were gathering themselves, too. What light there was caught Zach's light hair and the gold clasp of Audrey's Brunetti calfskin belt. Jenny could see by their faces that they knew Julian better now—not because they'd seen him in the Game but because they understood what he was.

Julian smiled his strange, sweet smile.

"You all wanted to know who I am. Well, I'll give you a final riddle," he said. "I'm a Visitor from the stars. I'm the Erlking. I'm Loki. I'm Puck. I'm the Hunter. I'm the Shadow Man. I'm your nightmares come true."

"We figured that out," Jenny said, quietly, steadily. "And we played your game and won. Now we want to go home."

"You didn't let me finish," Julian said, turning the smile on her. "Do you remember, when you first came in the game store, I showed you the ancient Tibetan game of goats and tigers?" He gestured, one of his easy, flowing motions, and Jenny saw the bronze board on a table. Tiny figures, also bronze, sat on it somewhat like chess pieces.

"Well, that's what you've really been playing," Julian said, and at the sound of his voice Jenny felt the walls closing in. He smiled at her particularly.

"You are all the innocent little goats . . . *and I'm the tiger.*"

Tom's hands were gripping Jenny's numbingly. Dee was in the forward stance, left leg forward, right leg back, ready for action. Zach looked bleak, and Audrey and Michael had moved closer together.

"You didn't really think," Julian said to Jenny, "that I would let you go."

Jenny felt dizzy. Smothering.

"You said . . . you were playing the Game fairly," she got out, with barely the breath to say it. "You promised me—"

"I'm not hidebound by tradition. And I *am* playing fairly—I said if you got to the turret before dawn, you'd find the door home standing open. It is open—it's just that I won't let you get to it."

Jenny looked at the animals guarding the door. What could even Dee do to fight them?

"By the way, *Tommy,* here, hasn't even faced his real nightmare yet. But there'll be plenty of time. We've got something like eternity ahead of us, you know," Julian said. His eyes were like liquid cobalt —and ravenous. Hungrier than the wolf's as he looked at Jenny and Tom together there.

God help me, Jenny thought. Please, *someone* help. She looked at Tom, but Tom was looking at Julian, with such hatred and fury that it made Jenny afraid for him.

"Then this whole 'Game' has been a farce," Tom said, almost spitting the words. His hazel eyes were burning.

Julian spread his hands and inclined his head slightly—almost a bow. As if someone had complimented him on a job well done. But it was Jenny he spoke to.

"I told you I'd do whatever was necessary to get you. At first I was sure you'd lose the Game—most people do. Then, when I saw you had a chance of winning, I figured I could make you turn to me for help. But you wouldn't. She's very strong, you know," he added, flicking a heavy-lidded glance at Tom. "Much too good for you."

"I know," Tom said, and Jenny looked at him, astonished. "But she's a thousand times too good for *you.*"

"I want her for goodness' sake," Julian said and smiled. "Light to my darkness. You'll see—Tommy. You'll have years and years and years to see how well she and I fit together." He turned back to Jenny. "In any case, you've gotten this far, and I'm afraid I have to tell you the truth. Which is that the whole Game has been just—a game. The kind a cat plays with a mouse."

"Before eating it?" Dee said in a voice like a knife.

Julian barely glanced back at her. "I'm only hungry for one thing at the moment, Deirdre. But my friends by the door have strange appetites. I wouldn't go near them if I were you. And of course there are all the other Shadow Men—all my elders, those ancient, bone-sucking, lip-licking wraiths—they'd all like to get hold of you. This house keeps them outside—but you wouldn't get far if you opened a window."

Jenny felt the trembling in Tom's clenched fists and bowed her head. She was thinking of the poem in her grandfather's room.

Like the other fools/Who've slipped on these same stones and played and lost . . .

Did everyone lose to the Shadow Men?

The dice are loaded, she thought. You can't win.

All bets are off.

"They'd love to sink a tooth in *you,*" Julian was saying to Dee. "Do you know you're the image of Ankhesenamun, one of the greatest beauties of Egypt?" Even as he spoke, Dee snapped her right leg up in a high kick, pulling her toes back at the last minute to deliver a devastating blow with the heel. At least, that was how it should have happened. Julian, with the reflexes of a rattlesnake, caught her foot as it came at him and jerked up, flinging Dee on her back.

"Rule One in this Game," Julian said, smiling. "Don't mess with me. I'll beat you every time."

Dee got up, obviously in pain—there was no way to break a fall like that—and Julian turned back to Jenny.

Jenny met his ravenous eyes and felt something inside her change forever.

"Let the others go," she said clearly and softly, "and I'll stay with you."

Julian stared at her. Everyone stared at her.

Then somebody—she thought it was Michael—started to laugh.

Julian smiled, very slightly, just one corner of his lip up. Not an amused smile. His eyes had gone the blue of gas flames.

"I see," he said.

Jenny detached her hands from Tom's. She stood up.

"I'm serious. Let them go . . . and I'll stay . . . of my own free will. And you know what that means." She was thinking of the darkroom, of the boy masquerading as her cousin who'd held her in his arms. The boy she'd *kissed*—of her own free will. She was hoping Julian remembered, too.

She thought he did. He looked intrigued. A strange, sensuous smile curved his lips.

"Willingly?" he repeated, as if testing the word.

"Willingly."

"No . . ." Tom whispered.

"Willingly," Jenny repeated, looking only at Julian.

Julian looked charmed—but wary. "You'd have to make a promise—seal the bond. In a way that couldn't be broken."

"Yes."

She could see she'd startled him. He'd expected her to play for time, to argue. Didn't he understand that she'd changed? She raised her eyebrows at him, ironically. "The sooner the better," she said.

Julian blinked, then said slowly, "Beautiful Deirdre can leave, and Audrey. So can Zach and Michael. But *Tommy* stays. I'll keep him as a hostage for your good behavior."

Looking up at him, Jenny felt her lip twitch, not quite a smile. "I don't think you'll need that. . . ."

"All the same."

"All right. It doesn't matter to me." Then, stepping close to him, she spoke quietly, for his ears alone. "Julian, don't you know that I've changed? Can't you *see* that? I still care about Tom, but . . . it's not the same. He'd seem tame after you. Anything would seem tame after you."

His eyes widened slightly in fascination.

Jenny took a deep breath. "I probably would have come to you a lot earlier if you'd just straight out asked me. Didn't that ever occur to you? That you could just appear at my front door, no games, no threats, and just *ask* me?"

He looked disconcerted. "Not exactly. . . ."

"You're too cynical. Do you know, I think the way you look at things has made you blind. You've gotten so hardened that you think you have to *fight* the universe to get what you want. To—sort of wrestle it out of people."

"And—don't I?"

"Not always," Jenny said. Meeting his gaze directly, she said, "Sometimes there's a much simpler solution. There are some things you can't force, Julian, and you can't buy them, either. They have to be *given,* for free. That's what I want to give you."

His fascination was complete.

"Then promise yourself to me," he said, and with a motion like a sleight-of-hand trick, he held something between his fingers. A gold circlet.

Jenny reached for it automatically, taking it between forefinger and thumb. It was a simple ring, with a design she couldn't quite make out on the outside. Inside the band something was written in fancy script. She tilted the ring toward one of the small lamps.

All I refuse & Thee I chuse, she read.

"Put this on your finger and you're sworn mine," Julian said. "No way to break the promise, no way to change the bond. It's a short ceremony. Do you want to go through with it?"

15

Yes," Jenny said.

Audrey gasped. "Jenny—for God's sake."

Jenny didn't look at her.

Tom made some movement. Jenny didn't look his way, either.

"Jenny . . ." Dee whispered. "It's not worth it. I know your promises—you keep them. You'll be *trapped*. Don't do it for us."

Jenny turned, then. She looked straight into the dark eyes with the slightly amber-tinted whites. "Dee . . . I'm sorry. I know you don't understand— and I can't explain it to you. But please believe me, I'm staying because I *want* to. Audrey, can't *you* understand?"

Audrey slowly shook her copper head, highlights flaring.

"I don't have a lot of real friends," she said. "I don't want to lose you."

"You're going to anyway," Jenny said. "This way is just easier on everyone. And I *want* to stay. I swear I do."

Dee had been staring at Jenny hard. Now, abruptly, her ebony face went blank. Walled off. Utterly without expression.

"That's right," she said. "You have to look out for number one." She nodded at Jenny, face grim, eyes meeting Jenny's directly. "Go ahead, Sunshine. Good luck."

Jenny nodded back. If it hadn't been manifestly impossible, she would have said the glitter in Dee's eyes was tears.

She turned back to Julian, who took the ring from her.

"A short ceremony," he said again. "Give me your hand."

A stained-glass lampshade threw blue and purple light over him. Jenny gave him her hand, felt that his was as cool as hers.

"Oh, don't," Audrey said, as if involuntarily.

Jenny didn't move.

"Seventeenth-century poesy ring, used to be given as tokens between lovers," Julian explained, holding up the gold circlet. "With the inscription on the inside. It means you refuse all the world except the one who gives it to you. The words touch your skin and bind you with their power."

Jenny smiled at him.

Tom stood slowly, his chains scraping up the sides of the clock with a sound like ball bearings rolling on wood.

Julian ignored everything but Jenny. "Now you

repeat after me. But remember—the promise is irrevocable." With a slight, grave formality, he said, as if quoting:

> "This ring, the symbol of my oath,
> Will hold me to the words I speak:
> All I refuse and thee I choose."

Jenny repeated the words and felt the cool band slide onto her finger. Then she looked at it. It shone with a rich, warm light, as if it had always been there.

"Now if we seal the bargain with a kiss, it becomes irrevocable," Julian said again, looking down at her. As if giving her a last chance to back out. The circlet burned on Jenny's finger like cold fire.

Jenny turned her face up. She didn't have to go far on tiptoe to kiss him. It was a soft kiss, but not a quick one.

Julian was the one who lifted his head from it.

"Sworn mine," he whispered. "Now and forever."

The violence came from an unexpected quarter.

"No," said Zachary, surging forward as if he was going to attack Julian.

Julian didn't even bother to look at him. Zach slammed into an invisible wall and fell back into Dee.

Jenny did turn, to look at all of them. Audrey and Zach and Dee and Michael. Her friends.

"I knew you wouldn't like this—" she began, but Zach interrupted her. He was on his feet again, gray eyes flashing in a way Jenny had never seen, face more intense than ever.

"How could you?" he burst out. He seemed as

angry on Tom's behalf as if he himself were being betrayed. "How *could* you?"

"Leave her alone," Michael said shortly. Jenny could see his opinion in his dark spaniel eyes—Mike thought she was making the best of a very bad situation. He didn't blame her for it. "What do you want her to do?" he said, and Zach shook his head in contempt.

"Not go willingly," he said. "Not give in—to that."

Tom was watching it all with blank eyes. Jenny could barely make herself look at him, but she did.

"I'm sorry, Tommy," she said. She saw his face twist slightly, and for a terrible moment she thought he was going to cry. Then he shrugged.

"I suppose it had to happen. That's the name of the Game, isn't it?" he said, looking at Julian.

Julian gave him an odd smile, and Jenny realized they were talking about something she didn't understand. "I keep my promises, too," he said. "All of them."

Jenny touched his sleeve. His face changed as he turned toward her, as if he were forgetting everyone else in the room.

"The ceremony's done," he said. "We're promised."

"I know." Jenny let out a deep breath. The ring made a little weight on her finger, but she felt very light, very free. She spoke calmly and casually, as if she were organizing a picnic or a redecorating project. Something that had to be done fast, but right.

"Let the others go now, Julian. I wish you'd let Tom go, too—but if not, can't you please make him more comfortable? I think in a few days you'll realize you don't need a hostage to keep me behaving."

He was searching her face, as if stricken by doubt for the first time. "Jenny—you really want to stay here? It's going to be strange for you. . . ."

"That is the understatement of the century." She looked up at him and spoke freely. "I only hope to God we can get a different view out the parlor window. But, yes, I want to stay. I never realized how much more there was to life than what I was getting. Now that I've seen it, I can't go back. I'm not the same person I was before."

He smiled. "No. In less than twelve hours you've changed. You've become . . ."

Jenny raised her eyebrows. "What?"

"I'll tell you later. I'll enjoy telling you, taking a long time to do it." He turned.

"You can all go." Jenny heard Tom's chains rattle and clank to the floor. Out of the corner of her eye, she saw him hold his hands up, free.

"Out!" Julian said with a snap of his fingers. For an instant Jenny thought he meant it for Dee and the others, but then the phantom wolf, which had been bristling, lowered its head and slunk off. Straight through the wall, apparently. The luminous snake slithered and poured itself through the floor. Some compartment in Jenny's mind noticed with awe how long that took, how much length there was to pour.

The door home stood open, unguarded. From this angle Jenny could see the rune Uruz on it, the inverted *U* flaring fire-red with power.

Through the door—and through the small window—she could see midnight blue. She glanced at the clock, which was still ticking away. 5:50 A.M.

Dawn was coming fast.

"Go on," Julian said, as if eager to be rid of them.

"Not without Jenny," Dee said.

Michael, Jenny thought, was surprised. He looked at Dee, opened his mouth. Zach's mouth was curled angrily. Audrey was shaking her head in doubt. Tom just stood.

Jenny looked away.

Julian's voice was impatient. "Well, go, stay, do whatever you want," he said. "I'll leave you to argue it out. But, remember, that door closes at dawn. Six-eleven sharp. If you're still inside, you're here for good—and I might not be in the mood for company."

He turned to Jenny. "This place is crowded."

"I know. There's a couch downstairs. We can sit on it and get acquainted."

They went.

The sofa in Jenny's grandfather's basement was shabby and lumpy but wide and very soft. It sank under their weight. Jenny found it odd to be sitting beside Julian like this, with no animosity, no need to pull away. No battles to fight.

It was a very private place. She knew the others wouldn't open the stairway door and come down, or even look in before they left the Shadow House. Julian's warning about not wanting company was sufficient. They all knew what he could do.

She looked up at him, to find him looking at her. So close. His eyes the color of a May morning.

Very deep, but very gentle.

She could feel his hunger.

And could feel herself trembling slightly. Her nerves jangling with excitement—and fear. But he didn't even touch her, at first. He just looked at her, with an expression she'd never seen on his face before. A look of wonder. The tenderness she'd seen when he was impersonating Zach.

"Are you frightened?" he said.

"A little." She was trying not to show it. She said lightly, "So you're the youngest Shadow Man."

"And the nicest."

"I believe that," Jenny said earnestly.

He did touch her, then, fingers light on her hair. Jenny felt the little inner stillness, the change in perception that comes before response. She shut her eyes and told herself not to think, not to feel anything but the featherlike touch. The lighter it was, the more it moved her.

She was surprised when it stopped. She opened her eyes—and was even more surprised at the anger in his face.

For an instant Jenny was *really* frightened, and the reality of what she was doing came home to her. Then she saw that Julian wasn't angry at her but—for her.

"You're so—innocent," he said. "That boyfriend of yours, that—*Tommy,* that spoiled, swaggering—he never thought about you, did he? Only about himself. And he botched it. I'd like to kill him."

This wasn't at all what Jenny wanted to think about. She started to say so, but Julian was going on, his eyes full of wild blue light.

"You want to watch out for that cousin of yours, too. He really does think about you, you know. I took that impression from life."

Knowing it was completely inappropriate, Jenny burst into slightly hysterical, but genuine laughter.

". . . you're jealous," she said, when she could get her breath. "Of *Zach*. Zach doesn't like people, only lenses and things."

The dark look disappeared from his face. "It doesn't matter," he said. "He won't be able to get at you here. No one will, ever. I'll keep you safe. . . ."

Jenny reached for him and lightly pressed her lips to his. He forgot about talking, then, and kissed back—such a soft kiss, his warm lips barely brushing hers.

But the soft kisses developed into slow shivery kisses and then into white-hot ones. She was still afraid of him, even as she clung to him—was it true that fear had to be a part of passion? Everywhere he touched she felt fire and ice.

Upstairs, the clock struck six.

Jenny pulled away from Julian, reluctantly. "I have to breathe," she whispered. She shook herself a little, then stood up. "Things are happening so fast."

He smiled as she walked around, getting her breath back, feeling her flushed cheeks cool. She couldn't look at him right now; she needed to regain her composure. Scarcely seeing it, she fingered the cobalt bracelet on the shelf.

"Why did you let me through my nightmare?" she said abruptly. "Sentimental reasons?"

"Not at all." He laughed. "I *did* play the Game fairly. I don't lie, even if I sometimes—withhold information. Your nightmare was remembering what happened that day. You couldn't see it, but the door appeared as soon as you remembered opening the closet."

"Oh," Jenny said softly. "The closet." Then she

added, "What did he want from you? My grandfather?"

"What everybody else wants. Power, knowledge— the easy way. A free ride."

"And runes really work," Jenny said, shaking her head slightly in wonder.

"A lot of things work. A lot of things don't. People can't tell which are which until they try them—and then they're usually surprised."

Jenny went over to the closet, looked inside. He followed, standing beside her.

"I'm sorry," Jenny said quietly, without looking at him. "I'm sorry he did it. He wasn't a bad man." Then she turned. "I can hardly believe he kept you here."

"Believe it," Julian said grimly.

Jenny shook her head. "I'll always love him. But he was wrong to do what he did." She stepped into the closet. "Not as small as it looks."

"Small enough." He stepped in, too, looked around. "This place brings up bad memories."

"See if we can't make a better one." She smiled up at him, backed up against one wall.

He turned and smiled down at her. In the confined space they were very close. Jenny stood shyly, one leg crossed behind the other.

He bent his head again, his mouth warm and demanding. Jenny gave herself up to it, and the kiss opened like a slow-blooming flower. Became so breathless and urgent that Jenny couldn't break it, even though she knew she had to. She kept thinking, Just one more minute, just one more minute . . .

It was Julian who pulled back.

"It's rather uncomfortable in here."

"Do you think so?" She smiled up at him, breath slowing.

"Definitely."

"Well, then, I suppose we could—"

Now, she thought.

In the middle of her sentence she moved. She had been standing in the cross stance, a kung fu stance Dee had taught her. Good for instant lateral movement. Now, in a split second, she used the power of her left leg to throw her to the right, vaulting out of the closet. In the same motion she slammed shut the door.

"Nauthiz!" she shouted. She slashed the *X* in the air.

As she shouted it, the rune flashed brightly on the closet door. Not red like fire, but blue-white like ice.

She didn't know if she was doing it right, but it was what her grandfather had done—or tried to do. Shut the door, trace the rune, say the name. She pronounced it as her grandfather had pronounced it.

And Julian did *not* come leaping out after her.

The closet door stayed closed.

The silence was deafening.

Jenny turned and ran for the staircase.

He lied, Jenny thought, racing up the steps. He changed the rules and he lied. Sometimes you can't return good for evil; sometimes evil simply has to be *stopped.*

She knew all this, of course; it had been in her mind from the very beginning, from the moment when she'd offered to stay with Julian. She didn't need to explain it to herself.

She was saying it to the whispering, plaintive voices in her own head that were begging her to go back.

Dawn tinted the turret window pink as she burst into the room. The door was a rectangle of pure palest rose with some lacy white clouds thrown in. The view was only slightly obscured by the five people standing around it.

Five. All of them. Dee, she'd expected—she knew Dee. Tom, she'd been worried about; she'd wanted him to understand, but she'd wanted him to leave even more. She'd hoped that Zach would be mad enough to go, and that Audrey would be sensible enough. Michael, she'd assumed, would be out like a shot.

"Go!" she shouted as she ran to them. She couldn't help glancing at the grandfather clock, which showed a scrolled minute hand leaning far too far past the ten. *"Go!"*

Tom's face had lighted with—well, with an expression that sent Jenny soaring the last five feet. "Go on!" he said to the others, reaching for Jenny.

It wasn't as easy a proposition as it sounded. There was nothing outside this door. No Ice Age, no living room. Nothing but dawn. Stepping out into that took guts.

"Oh, what the hell," said Michael, and, holding hands with Audrey, he took the step.

Dee flashed a barbaric grin over her shoulder and jumped out like a skydiver.

Zach was the one who balked. Jenny couldn't believe it. "Where is he?" Zach demanded.

"In the closet. Go, go!"

Zach's face was still dark. "I thought you meant it—"

Tom gave him a good straight-arm shove, running-back style. Zach fell out sprawling, spinning, arms and legs extended.

It didn't look like fun. They were trusting to fate. No—to Julian, a much more dangerous proposition. Trusting that when he'd said Jenny's friends could leave, he had meant alive.

And trusting to Grandpa Evenson, Jenny thought, that the rune of containment would contain. Tom reached to take her hand in both of his. The sky was a blaze of rose and gold.

They looked at each other and stepped out that way, together.

They were falling as the sun appeared. In that instant the entire sky around them turned a color Jenny had seen only once before. An unbelievable luminous blue, the color of Julian's eyes.

No matter how often you faint, you never really get used to it. Jenny came to herself slowly. She was lying down, she knew that first. Lying on something cool and very hard.

Mexican paver tiles.

She sat up much too fast and almost fainted again.

The first thing she saw was the Game.

It was sitting in the middle of her mother's solid ponderosa pine coffee table. The white box lid was on the floor beside the table. The rune Uruz was dull as rust.

The Victorian paper house itself was tall and

219

perfect, its printed colors richly glowing in the rosy eastern light. The only difference Jenny could see was that the slips of paper they'd drawn their nightmares on were gone—as were the paper dolls they'd drawn of themselves.

It all looked so innocent, so wholesome, with the Tupperware tub of Joey's crayons sitting beside it.

"Maybe it was all a dream," Michael said hoarsely.

He was on the other side of the table, with Audrey, who was just straightening up. Her glossy auburn hair was windblown into a lion's mane. It made her look quite different, quite—free.

"It wasn't a dream," Dee said with uncharacteristic quietness, uncoiling her long legs and standing. "Summer's gone."

Zach picked himself up and sat on a leather footstool. He said nothing, but rubbed his forehead as if his head hurt.

Jenny looked at Tom.

He was sitting up very slowly, using the table as help. Jenny put a hand under his arm, and he looked a "thank you" at her. He'd changed. Maybe even more than Audrey. He looked battered and sore, and he'd lost his air of always being in control. There was a new expression in his eyes, a sadness that was almost grateful at the same time. Jenny didn't know the word for it.

Maybe something like *humility*.

"Tommy," she said, worried.

The rakish smile was crooked. Battered as his devilish good looks. "I thought maybe you were really staying with him. To save me—and because you wanted to. And the thing was, I wouldn't have blamed you. I sort of realized that when he gave you the ring."

Jenny, who had been about to protest, looked at her hand. Any lingering doubts about last night being real were shattered. It was there, shining on her finger.

"I thought *definitely* you really were staying with him," Audrey said. "You had me convinced you honestly wanted to—and it was all a trick?"

"It was the truth. I *was* doing it of my own free will, and I did want to stay—long enough to make sure Tom and you guys got out."

"*I* knew," Dee said.

"It's those brains of yours again," Jenny said, looking straight at her.

"And I always thought you were such a sweet little thing," Michael was musing. "So simple, so honest . . ."

"I am—when people treat me fairly. When they don't kill my friends. When they don't break their word. I figured he made up the rules of that game, and trickery was a legal move. So I did it."

Audrey persisted. "And you really never felt anything for him? That was all an act?"

"Just call me Sarah Bernhardt," Jenny said.

She hoped that Audrey wouldn't notice she hadn't answered the question.

"Who cares?" Michael said. "We're home. We did it." He looked around at the sunlight flooding in through the sliding glass door, at the ordinary Thornton backyard outside, at the pastel walls of the living room. "I love each and every one of these baskets," he said. "I could kiss the tiles we sit on. I could kiss *you*, Audrey."

"Oh, if you have to," Audrey said, not bothering to fuss with her hair. She leaned forward and so did Michael.

Dee, though, was still looking at Jenny, her night-dark eyes serious. "What about the betrothal?" she said. "The ring? You're supposed to be promised to him now."

"What about it?" Jenny said quietly. "I'm going to throw the ring away. With the rest of this garbage."

In a single motion that brought Zach's head up, she crushed the paper house, smashing it flat and flatter. She put it in the white box, like filling an overstuffed suitcase, pushing it in where it wouldn't fit. She scooped up the game cards and jammed them in, too.

Then she took the ring off. It came quite easily, not sticking to her finger or anything. She didn't look at the inscription.

She dropped the ring on top of it all.

Then she put in the paper dolls of the Creeper and the Lurker. As she picked up the third doll she paused.

It was the boy with the shocking blue eyes.

They seemed to be looking up at her, but she knew they weren't. It was just a tagboard cutout, and the original was locked away under a rune of constraint that would hold, she hoped, forever.

She hadn't let go of the Shadow Man doll yet.

It was your Game. You hunted us. You told me to become a hunter. You just never expected to be trapped yourself.

What would this world be like without a Julian in it? Safer, certainly. Calmer. But poorer, too, in a way.

She'd beaten the Shadow Man, but it was strangely hard to consign him to oblivion. Jenny felt a pang of something oddly like regret, of something lost forever.

She put the doll in the box and crammed the lid on.

There was a roll of masking tape in with Joey's crayons. Jenny wound tape round and round the bulging white box, sealing it shut. The others all watched in silence.

When she finally ran out of tape she put the box on the table and sat back on her heels. A smile began somewhere in the group and traveled from one person to another. Not a partying kind of smile, just one of quiet relief and joy. They had made it. They'd won. They were alive—most of them.

"What are we going to say about Summer?" Tom asked.

"We're going to tell the truth," Jenny said.

Audrey's eyebrows arched. "No one will ever believe us!"

"I know," Jenny said. "We're going to tell them anyway."

"It'll be all right," said Dee. "After all we've been through, we can deal with it. As long as we're all together."

"We are," Jenny said, and Tom nodded. In the old days—last night—it would have been the other way around.

Audrey and Michael, who couldn't seem to separate from each other, both nodded, too. So did Zach, who was for once paying attention to the rest of them, instead of being off in his own little world.

I think it actually helped him, Jenny thought suddenly, to know that his grandfather was only calling up demons and not insane after all.

"We can call the police from the kitchen," she said aloud.

16

It was Dee who made the phone call, because Audrey and Michael were looking out the kitchen window together, and Zach wasn't the talking type. Jenny and Tom had moved a little away from the others.

"I wanted to show you this," Tom said.

It was a tattered scrap of paper. It had several things drawn and then crossed out—Jenny thought one was a rat. The only thing not crossed out was in the middle, and Jenny couldn't tell what it was.

"I'm a rotten artist. I thought you could tell by the yellow hair and green eyes."

"I'm your worst nightmare?" Jenny said, only half joking because she was completely bewildered.

"No. It was hard to draw, but it was what I meant at the end when I told Julian I guessed it had to happen. The name of the Game was face your worst nightmare, and that was mine. Losing you."

Jenny could only look at him.

"I'm not good at saying it. Maybe I'm not even

good at showing it," he said. "But—I love you. As much as he does. More."

All Jenny could think of was hibiscus bushes. Little Tommy in second grade. The boy she had decided she was going to marry—on sight.

Something was tugging at her inside, but she knew she had to put it—even the memory of it—away forever. Never think of it again. And never let Tom know.

Never.

"I love you, too," she whispered. "Oh, Tom, so much."

It was at that moment they heard the glass break.

Dee was hampered by being on the phone. Tom was hampered by Jenny. The others were just plain frozen.

Still, it was only a few seconds before they ran back to the living room, just in time to see two figures ducking out the broken sliding glass door with really astonishing speed.

The white box wasn't on the coffee table anymore.

Tom and Dee, of course, ran into the backyard. But even Jenny, standing by the broken door, could see there was no chance. The two figures were over the wall and gone before their pursuers got close. After climbing the block wall and looking around, Tom and Dee came slowly back.

"They just disappeared," Dee said in disgust.

"They were *flying*," Tom panted.

"You're not in the best of shape, either of you," Jenny said. "It doesn't matter. I didn't really want to give the Game to the police anyway. It probably won't work for anyone else."

"But who *were* they? Shadow Men?" Michael asked.

"Shadow Men in sneakers," Dee said, pointing to a muddy footprint on the tiles.

"But why would they *want* to—"

Jenny tuned him out. She was looking at the broken glass and trying not to think. Even from behind, those two guys had looked familiar.

But surely what she'd said was true. The Game had been meant for her; it shouldn't work for anyone else. Besides, it was squashed now, ruined. And even if it did work for someone else, what were the chances of them making it all the way up to the third floor, into her grandfather's basement? And even if they did make it there, what were the chances of them opening a white closet door?

"Good riddance to it," Tom said. In the early morning light his dark hair shone, and the green flecks in his eyes looked gold. "Everything I care about is right here," he said. He smiled at Jenny. "No more nightmares," he told her, with open love in his face, in front of them all.

Jenny went into the circle of his arms.

In a vacant lot, two boys were panting, looking behind them for pursuers.

"I think we lost them," said the one in the black bandanna and T-shirt.

"They weren't even trying," said the one in the black-and-blue flannels.

They looked at each other in a mixture of triumph and fear.

They didn't know what the box was, despite a night of watching the blond girl's house. It hadn't been until dawn that they'd worked up the nerve to break in—and then the white box had been there on the table, waiting for them.

They knew only that ever since seeing it they'd been compelled to follow it, fearing it and wanting it in equal measure. It had dominated their thoughts, sending them after the girl, keeping them up all night.

And now they had it, at last.

One of them flicked out a knife and slit the tape.

About the Author

LISA JANE SMITH realized she wanted to be a writer sometime between kindergarten and first grade. She got the idea for her first published book while baby-sitting in high school, and wrote it while attending the University of California at Santa Barbara (in between classes, of course).

Dreams and nightmares have always fascinated her. Many of her books, including *The Forbidden Game* trilogy, are based on her own nightmares and those of her friends. At times she stops in the middle of a particularly frightening dream and thinks, "This is awful. I sure hope I remember it when I wake up!"

She lives in a rambling house in the Bay Area of northern California with one dog, three cats, and about ten thousand books.

Look for the next exciting book in
THE FORBIDDEN GAME trilogy:

VOLUME II: *THE CHASE*

One by one, Jenny's friends are disappearing—
with paper dolls left in their places. Julian has
returned with a new game of terror to make
Jenny his own. His hunting companions are the
Lurker, a ghostly wolf, and the Creeper, a phantom snake. Can Jenny save her friends and
win . . . or will she become Julian's prize?